I

1.

I can remember quite clearly the day my parents died. I must've been seven years old, or in seventh grade, one of those two (I don't remember). In any event, that's probably not the best way to start a story if the reader is to believe the words that follow! But there was always something about the number seven…

Seven, while considered a lucky number by many, for reasons which I sincerely doubt anyone truly understands, has always portended quite the opposite for me – The seven seas I would sail as a merchant mariner later in life, a voyage I will recount for the reader's sake (certainly not my own); seven "deadly" sins I would commit over and over again in the vain hope that the invisible man upstairs would one day make good on his promise to strike me down; seven carriages of fire and steel that would pile up on my parents and sister as they drove along Interstate 77 on their way home from Cleveland, OH to XXXXXXXXXX, XX.

"Father, shouldn't you slow down a little?"

"Like Hell, Mother!"

Like Hell indeed.

Not that any of the other numbers have done me much better in this life. When you've lived to be as old as I have, every factor, equation, and sum conceived of since the time of Pythagoras (nay, since the advent of the Mayan zero!) comes to represent some tragedy or another, if you let it. Then again, it is doubtful that one even has a choice in this regard, once you've lived to be my age.

2.

It was shortly after the funeral that I was sent to live with a man and woman claiming to be my aunt and uncle, though I had no recollection of ever having met them, or even having heard of their existence up until then. Apparently, however, they had the documentation to prove it, and since that was really all it took, no amount of protest on my part was going to prevent the adoption.

Besides, where else was I going to live?

Therefore, in the absence of other viable options, it only made sense that I went to live with them. So I went

Editorial

to live in their house, a rather typical looking house that had evidently been painted peach pink once a long time ago. Now though, it more closely resembled the pale, grey hide of a dead or dying animal. It was a medium-sized house on a rather tall hill, somewhere in the western central United States. The view, however, was remarkably short in whichever direction one looked.

Most of my time was spent reading and masturbating in my room, activities which seem equally self indulgent in retrospect. Hours of page-peeling and penis-pumping (and sometimes penis-peeling and page-pumping, when things got really out of hand) were punctuated only by mealtimes, when I would descend the stairs to eat with the strangers who presumably read, slept, and pleasured themselves in the room down the hall from mine.

Mealtimes with aunt and uncle were always an incredibly interesting, if dreadfully dull affair. At three regularly spaced intervals throughout the day, we would gather around the modest dining room table, where we would put various nondescript edible items into our mouths and down our throats for later passage to the toilet.

It wasn't that aunt was a particularly bad cook, she just wasn't very imaginative. In fact, the only way I could tell the difference between breakfast, lunch, and dinner was by observing the behavior of those providing my board. For instance, I could always tell that it was breakfast time when uncle would ignore the food in front of him, opting to place a newspaper between it, us, and himself for the duration of the meal instead (before hurrying out the door and off to work). Lunchtime came when only aunt and I were present at the table, and just in case I forgot that uncle never came home for lunch, working far away as he did, aunt would always make sure to weep quietly across the table from me, so as to prevent any upsetting confusion.

One could usually tell when it was dinnertime by the piercing shrieks and deafening bellows that would emit from aunt and uncle, respectively. These periodic outbursts were sometime punctuated by long periods of silence, but occasionally their alternating high and low frequencies would reverberate throughout the entire meal without pause.

A clatter of seething silver in the sink.

Every once in a great while there would come a dinner (I think) devoid of all such shouts, screams, and silences, sometime with strange, soft words spoken in their place, which upset and bewildered me greatly at first. But over time I learned to associate these disturbing scenes with another dinner, or should I say *post*-dinner convention.

After dinners where no shrieking or bellowing took place at the table at all, either aunt or uncle would place a record onto the old-fashioned player in the parlor, lock hands with one another, and proceed to step, spin, and dip around the room in time to the shrieking and bellowing sounds which issued forth from the speakers. Though it pained me to watch their grotesque displays – bodies and faces moving and contorting in such unnatural ways – this at least helped me to determine whether I had just eaten dinner or some queasily unfamiliar new meal that I'd now have to get used to. The sound of that shrieking and bellowing, whether coming from the mouths of aunt and uncle or from the mouth of the Victrola, always came as quite a relief.

3.

This need for routine and familiarity – my abhorrence of all things new and strange – would mark the central theme of my formative years, and would follow me well into adulthood and beyond as well. It never even occurred to me that my days of reading and masturbating in my room all day (and being coaxed downstairs three times each 24 hours for my daily sustenance) would ever come to an end.

Then one day around the time I was seventeen, or maybe twenty-four, I was enjoying a typically bland, boring, perfectly delightful lunch with aunt when she gave me good reason to suspect that it wasn't lunchtime after all. It was at that moment that I noticed, with some disconcertion, that she was weeping slightly louder than usual. So I said to her:

"Aunt, whatever is the matter?"

To which she responded, through ever-thickening tears, "Today... nephew, is the day... you leave us."

I was flabbergasted. I was speechless. I couldn't tell if it was the thoroughly bizarre sounds that aunt now insisted on making – like her usual sobbing, only deeper and more guttural – or the prospect of "leaving" that had me most out of sorts. Leave? Where on Earth could I possibly *leave* to? There wasn't a visible point of destination for miles around in any direction, save for the spot on the horizon where the winding single lane which began at our drive entered the oblivion between the dust in the air and the dust on the ground.

Determined to thwart her awful prophecy at any cost, I threw down my fork with uncommon violence and stormed upstairs, where I intended to lock myself in my room and masturbate until dinnertime, by which time aunt would surely have come to her senses. Imagine my surprise, then, when my attempt to restore a much-needed sense of normalcy to my life was further impeded by none other than uncle, standing in the hall beside my bedroom door. At first I was too confused by his mere presence to even notice the suitcase and knapsack lying at his feet. So I said to him:

"Uncle, what is all this?"

To which he replied, through an ever-broadening grin, "Today, nephew, is the day that you leave us!"

I scarcely had time to protest before the bags were thrust into my hands and I was ushered out the front door, where I was left standing in unfamiliar territory upon the sagging planks of the front porch. An instant later I heard the door lock behind me.

Editorial

So, with a suitcase full of books in one hand and a knapsack containing a few toiletries, food items, and articles of clothing in the other, I did the only thing I was capable of doing at that moment, though it ran against every fiber of my being: I set a course for that dot on the horizon where the roiling dust above met the rolling dust below.

4.

I had not made it more than a quarter mile down the road before my left arm grew tired from the weight of the portable library in my suitcase. Having never had cause to pick up more than a book or two at a time, it never occurred to me just how heavy mere paper could be. At any rate, my frail arm soon grew numb while I pondered this paradox, and at length I was forced to set the suitcase down. Finding the rest of my body similarly fatigued, I decided to sit myself down along with it.

At this point the reader may be wondering just what kind of books I'd been reading all this time, which I'd been lugging along of late and only recently found myself sitting upon. Well, perhaps it will suffice to say that they weren't the kind of books you'd find at your local library.

No, that won't suffice at all... Alright then, out with it!

The books in question, each without exception, in fact, were exclusively pornographic in subject matter. Come to think of it, since they contained very few words to speak of (being composed primarily of nude photographs as they were), and since their covers were just slightly thicker than their pages (another reason why I was surprised at their weight), perhaps it isn't accurate to call them books at all. They were more like magazines. Yes, *dirty* magazines.

Honestly, I'm surprised you're so surprised. You didn't think I was up there rubbing myself raw to Faulkner, did you?

So there I sat, a veritable cornucopia of porn overflowing from beneath me, like a geyser of onanistic orgasmic potential, and with a decided paucity of privacy in which to enjoy it. Oddly enough, though, for the first time in my life I no longer felt like abusing myself in that manner. At the time I could barely feel anything, oblivious even to the billowing clouds of dust that were beginning to whip across the high desert plateau. Though I was hardly cognizant of it then, my skin began to take on the irregular yellow and brown pattern of the many reptile species native to the area – the finer, lighter grains of sediment adhering to the patches most drenched in sweat, while the darker, coarser component formed thicker layers over the less dampened zones.

A few times I thought I spied headlights approaching through the darkening distance, like snake eyes winding towards me from far on down the road. I suddenly felt the inexplicable urge to consume a raw egg whole, shell and all.

Slithering amongst the harsh landscape of cacti, sagebrush, and yucca, sliding on one's belly with ease across the hot sands and sharp stones that cover the wastelands between the wastelands – this is a markedly

Editorial

more pleasurable experience when one's soft, vulnerable skin has given way to hard, unfeeling scales.

To see the world from such an ideal vantage point – in a position to bite it in the ankle while simultaneously looking up its skirt – to know the land on such intimate terms, caressing every inch of its surface while at the same time delving into its deepest orifice… Perhaps this is the true reason why the snake has earned the collective scorn (or perhaps envy) of the human race. While the presumed masters of the planet search for salvation in the clouds, or admire the "nobler" animals who've broken their bounds to the earth and taken to the sky (where they live chained), the true masters are always underfoot and ready to strike at our most vulnerable points. And mankind has not forgotten it, if a popular fable found within a certain holy book is any indication…

5.

I have no way of knowing just how much time I spent sidewinding through the dry, desolate domains of the country, outside the towns and cities which – while equally arid in their own right – contained far too many instances of community and compassion (however few) to fully suit the cool, calculating nature of the reptilian heart and mind. Granted, that didn't stop many a snake in human guise from becoming prominent figures in the realms of man, but for the biological reptile, there was no question for them where they belonged.

At least I learned as much in my time as a snake.

When at last I regained my original form, I found myself nude and sprawling in the weeds behind an isolated truck stop about a hundred miles outside of Reno, Nevada. There I observed in the dust beside me the perfectly preserved moltings of a large rattler. It gave me no end of amusement to imagine the look on the faces of whoever discovered my *man* moltings, draped across a treasure trove of tits and ass, there on the dusty roadside where I'd left it.

In all likelihood, they'd only find my clothes...

Standing on one's own two feet, an act taken for granted by most, becomes much more of an imposition when one hasn't attempted it in a while. We know this to be true of people who come out of comas. But it wasn't so much an atrophy of leg muscles as it was a sickening

Editorial

vertigo that nearly forced me back down to a seemingly safer altitude.

Resisting the urge to cover the distance remaining between myself and the truck stop on my belly, I staggered in serpentine motion to the rubbish heap beside its back door, hoping to regain my balance and something suitable with which to cover myself. As luck would have it, there she was – a ragged blue tarp covering some rusty old engine parts, which I promptly took around my shoulders as a makeshift cloak of sorts. I didn't have to examine my reflection in the cracked windowpane, propped against the wall, to realize how foolish I must've looked.

Of all the different species on this planet, of which there are very many (hundreds of thousands counting insects and microorganisms alone), *Homo sapiens* – the so-called "wise ape" – is the only one that bothers to cover its ass. It is also the only species that purposefully poisons its own environment and murders its own kind *en masse*.

The reader may draw their own conclusions.

My first impulse was to walk into the truck stop stark naked, leaving the tarp to do a more important job – protecting the already ruined engine parts. But, upon further consideration (mainly of the fact that I hadn't eaten for a week and my metabolism was starting to catch up), I decided that it would be more expedient to my immediate goal if I entered the diner opposite the hotel rooms and showers wearing something more than just my scales (I mean skin).

6.

As can be expected anywhere people customarily gather, the "Oasis" truck stop (a mere metaphor of an establishment) was populated primarily by two types of people: Those who appeared happy to be there, telling jokes and making small talk with strangers, and those who were too road-bitten, too sullen for their obliged appearance, to even bother with the act. Usually these types sat at separate tables, though often they occupied the very same seat.

The odor of stale cigarette smoke and the sound of country western music (making the smoke seem fresh by comparison) permeated the atmosphere inside. A couple of cowboy types sat silently at a nearby table, apparently locked in a contest to see who could remain silent the longest. An ugly man and woman and their doubly ugly children (what happens when ugly multiplies) sat continuously yammering at another.

Despite the collection of fully functional antique clocks displayed along one wall, there was nothing in the diner to provide the slightest clue of what time it was or which meal was currently taking place. None of the dishes set before any of the other patrons were of much help either – each of them looked, smelled, and probably tasted exactly the same (perhaps even more so than aunt's uninspired fair).

Without thinking I sat down at the counter and ordered two eggs from the man on the other side of it. The worn, weathered tarp between my buttocks and the stool supporting them still had some crinkle left in it, I noticed, as I shifted my weight back and forth. No one in the diner

Editorial

seemed to notice anything beyond the confines of their peninsula-like booths and islandesque tables.

All but one. As I sat there in my crinkling kimono, eagerly awaiting the arrival of my sustenance, I became keenly aware of the attention I was receiving from a man three stools down from me. He was balding, bespectacled, and wearing a cheap brown and yellow checkered coat. He'd evidently been enjoying a cup of coffee alone when I first made the scene.

When at last he could be certain that he'd caught my attention as well, he engaged me in a peculiar dialogue (monologue was more like it) wherein he made obvious statements about things like the weather and asked me the most bizarre personal questions in between sips of coffee. I rarely responded.

"So where ya from kid?"

Though hardly a difficult question to answer in retrospect, I must admit that at the time it gave me considerable trouble. Not entirely sure how to answer, I responded with the first piece of half-formed thought that came into my head.

"Back over them there mountains," I told him, making a vague gesture to (what I thought was) the west, reasonably sure that I hadn't lied to him.

In any event, this admission on my part, rather than appeasing his curiosity (as I'd hoped) produced the completely opposite effect. Whereas his inquiries had once been punctuated by sips of coffee and short opportunities for response, they now came in relentless rapid-fire succession.

"So you're a Colorado boy, are ya? Or Utahan? You know I got a good buddy out there helluva guy!

What brings you to these parts anyway haven't you got any clothes to wear son?"

Luckily, I was spared from having to reply to so many questions at once by the arrival of my eggs. Only there was a problem – the eggs had been cracked open and *cooked*.

"That'll be $1.25," said the man behind the counter.

Somehow realizing that there were no pockets anywhere in my tarp, and no likely place to keep money anywhere else on my person, the man in the brown and yellow checkered coat quickly slid a crisp fiver across the counter.

"Don't worry," he said, apparently (and foolishly) concerned that I might object.

"It's on me."

7.

Outside in the parking lot, the man rummaged through the debris which filled the way-back of his brown and yellow station wagon, eventually coming out with an extra set of clothes identical to the set he wore, complete with a matching brown and yellow checkered coat.

"Might be a little big on you, but these should do," he said.

I changed in the car while the man checked something under the hood. At once I felt claustrophobically constricted by my new attire. Despite being two sizes too large, the man's clothes seemed to grip me like a vice compared to the tarp I'd been wearing and the snakeskin before that. For the first leg of the trip to Reno I could scarcely move at all without fear of bursting at the seams. When the man would ask me more of his questions I could only answer in short, swift exhalations, as I was having difficulty breathing by this point as well, you see.

By the time we reached the halfway point I was beginning to feel somewhat better. Also I had gotten to know the man a bit better as well, since he'd apparently asked all of the questions he wished to ask me, or simply lost interest in his role as interrogator and began to admit things about himself instead.

He was a traveling salesman by trade, and by his own account he'd peddled his wares (whatever they were) all up and down the west coast, making the trip from Anchorage to Acapulco and back again, as he put it:

"*Many* a time… *many* a time…"

He had an ex-wife and two children, whom he never phoned or visited, back east somewhere.

He, like many other American men of his generation, was very interested in and enthusiastic about football.

It was a good thing that he *did* tell me this last part, offhandedly as he did, otherwise I might've been surprised when he pulled off to the side of the road and ask me to touch his balls with my feet. Honestly I had been expecting it after his last remark, and if I hadn't, I would've found myself in the intolerably awkward position of having to ask him what he was thinking.

I will not recount for the reader what followed. If I must be forced to live without pornography, then so must you!

Let's just say that it involved the violent and repetitive upward and downward motion of one body working upon another, followed closely by a smooth transaction of warm bodily fluid and cold, hard cash.

Now that I think of it, this was the easiest money that I ever made in my entire life (keeping in mind that I've lived a very, very long time). This wouldn't dawn on me until many years later, after I'd become a much more worldly individual, but it seems to me now that the primary reason why prostitution remains such a despised occupation is plain and simple jealousy. After all, a good and efficient whore, even of the streetwalking variety, can easily make $80 an hour (one $40 lay and two $20 blowjobs, each act averaging about twenty minutes after the necessary prep-work and cleanup).

That's more money than most people can expect to make in an entire eight hour day! Granted, a hooker may face greater dangers than the average shift worker, and they may be forced to endure the unsavory stigma associated with their trade, but who *wouldn't* want to earn upwards of $80 an hour, just for doing what they were probably going to do anyway?

$40 + $20 + $20 = $80

Editorial

After all, we're all selling our time and labor to someone. Whether it's mouths on the phone and hands on the keyboard, or hands on the cock and mouths on the balls, the only real difference between these modes of employment is the length of time and amount of effort required to do a good job and earn a good wage. No wonder (the latter sort of) prostitutes are so widely despised...

It might make more sense for us all to start sucking each other off for our goods and services, as this would cut out the middleman and save everyone a boatload of time – time that could be spent on introspective contemplation, advancing the arts and sciences, or simply relaxing or having fun with our poor neglected friends and family.

I wonder if the world's various churches – some of the most vehement opponents of this "immoral" profession – are even aware that priest, priestess, and prostitute were once all one and the same.

Probably. Probably not. Doesn't matter.

8.

The greenish grey color of the sky and the heavy scent of ozone in the air portended rain (or worse) as we pulled into town. My first order of business was to find a cheap room for the night, which I managed to do with some ease, seeing as how I'd been through Reno on business so many times before.

Inside the lobby I reached into the breast pocket of my brown and yellow checkered coat and produced several crumpled bank notes that I'd earned along the way (glad that I now *had* pockets in which to keep such things), placing them on the counter just as I heard the sky open up over the town. I received my key and followed the clerk's directions to my room, listening to the violence of the storm picking up outside.

The room was small and sparsely furnished, but dry and comfortable nevertheless. I set my bags down next to the bed, undressed and began going over the list of Reno businesses and individuals whom I was scheduled to make calls to the following day:

Greyson School for Boys	(order)
Michael Michaelson	(order)
Brett Castle & Associates	(order)
Mendel Bottling Co.	(order)
Reno Medical	(order)
Reno City Hospital	(demonstration)
Sheila Langers	(demonstration)
Jolly-Freeze Ice Cream	(demonstration)
Pat Rosenburg	(delivery)
Durango, Inc.	(delivery)
Big Jack	(courtesy call)

I quickly planned my order of attack with the help of the city map in the phonebook (which I wouldn't have needed at all, if it weren't for all the new customers I'd acquired recently). With luck, it seemed, I could have all of my calls complete by mid-afternoon. Then I'd have time to see the show that was playing downtown, which Big Jack had personally recommended himself.

Either way I would be very busy tomorrow, and intended to get an early start. After draping the windows with the bedspread and unplugging the red glare of the

Editorial

alarm clock (for even the slightest light makes it impossible for me to sleep), I removed the remainder of my clothing and settled into bed, despite the fact that it was only half past seven.

Finding myself less tired than I'd expected, I decided to click on the television set and catch the early news.

> *...in the Persian Gulf today... another 217 civilians... Red Cross... rubble... White phosphorous shells... hospital... family members search for survivors amongst charred...*

With some interest I surveyed the awful scene as it unfolded. As the conventionally attractive young man and woman related the tragic events from earlier in the day (all the earlier for being so many time zones behind), I kept my eyes glued to the images of smoke, flames, emergency vehicles and weeping faces, oblivious now to the words coming out from in between their perfect white teeth. And then...

> *...in other news...*

Shit. Such a fucking *tease*. Not even a mangled limb; not so much as the suggestion of a single blackened corpse. I must admit that I had given myself quite a hard-on just thinking about the carnage they described – this despite the fact that I'd had my last orgasm less than two hours before.

In the end I decided to abstain from jerking off and went straight to sleep after my erection had subsided.

In the night I dreamt of rolling in a pile of sexless, smoldering Iraqis. In the morning I woke up in a puddle of my own black, oily jissom.

9.

Reno had become a real bitch to navigate since I'd last visited. Being the cooler time of year – the time most conducive to performing manual labor outside without shriveling like a grape in the sun – it seemed as if half the streets were in the process of either being dug up or filled in, and in some cases both simultaneously. As a result of this mayhem and the congested traffic which ensued, I didn't even make my first call until 9AM.

In kitchens and in boardrooms across the city, I would take my orders, do my demonstrations, and make my deliveries. If it were an order I was taking, I would take out my order book, lick my pencil tip, and say:

"What'll it be sir/ma'am?"

OR:

"What can I get for you today?"

Sometime either before or afterwards, I would usually hear "So how's your family?" or "What took ya so goddamned long?" depending on whether I was in someone's office or living room, respectively. I wasn't sure which I appreciated less – the insincere concern or the genuine indifference.

Editorial

If I were doing a demonstration, I would arrange my various satchels and cases upon coffee tables and desktops, open them, and removing various articles from their velvet and foam rubber entrails, I would say:

"Now these are from our latest line…"

OR:

"Perhaps I could interest you in this…"

These entreaties on my part would be met with varying degrees of success and failure, but the one constant, the one part of the transaction that I could always count on, was the well-concealed disgust and resentment on the part of both parties involved.

If I were delivering an order, which meant at least not *all* of my headaches and frustrations had been in vain, I'd usually be forced to sit in someone's waiting room or out on their patio – or on one occasion in a derelict bar on the outskirts of Omaha – wiling away the minutes and the hours of my day while so and so went on and on about such and such, offering me such useless items as cigarettes and soft drinks, and boring me half to death (if *only* all the way) with their incessant chatter, when all I really wanted was the payment I was due, so I could be off to the next town and the next blowjob/piece of ass/whatever else it had to offer.

It was around 11PM when I finally finished with my orders, demonstrations, and deliveries. All that was left was my courtesy call to Big Jack.

The lights had just gone down on the late show at the Desert Rose theatre when I found a seat at the rear of the darkened picture. Several indistinct forms were spread throughout the aisles, shuffling their feet and coughing nervously as I made my presence known, as if they thought they were in their own private booths or something.

Well, there *were* no private booths at the Desert Rose. If people wanted private booths, they could go to the Pussy Willow across town. Some people, like me, preferred a more public venue for their courtesy calls...

Young, smooth bodies, or at least the suggestion of them, so unlike my own reflection, jerk and glide across each other on the screen before me as I undo my belt and trousers.

"Well hello, Jack" I say, shaking his hand vigorously as he stands up to greet me.

"How ya been?"

10.

A man sits in a cubicle of grey, unadorned walls, computer terminal and telephone close at hand on the otherwise bare desk before him.

He begins the work of editing the book he's been assigned. A few additions, deletions, and modifications later, he lifts up the telephone receiver and attempts to reach the author with some questions he has regarding some proposed changes. Reaching only the author's answering service, he explains into the machine on the other end that he has some questions regarding the proposed changes.

Editorial

The editor then sets down the receiver and makes the proposed changes without further question, knowing that the answers will not come until well after the book is already in print, at which point it will be far too late for them (or their futile, yet inevitable protests) to make a single lick of difference.

"We've got *deadlines* to meet here!" he can hear his boss screaming, "You keep those edits MOVING, goddamnit!"

He takes his hands from the keyboard and considers the clock on the grey wall beyond his work station (its sole decoration), pleased to have jerked a few more dollars off of his employer's pendulous payroll account. He was certain that he would be fired within the week, probably any day now, a certainty he'd held on to since his initial hire two and a half years ago. He was determined to milk that clock for all it was worth in the meantime.

Then, giving a quick glance over both of his shoulders, he slides a small black imitation leather book out from its hiding place beneath his desk, places it next to some hard copy that needed going over yesterday, opens it up and begins to write:

> *The year is 2484 CE, 500 years to the day*
> *I was orphaned and sent to live with aunt*
> *and uncle…*

…in a house on a hill in the northwest corner of New Mexico (or was it the southwest corner of Wyoming?). Though many centuries had passed since that fateful day and the beginning of my even more fateful exodus, mankind and the world it inhabited had not changed as much as popular science fiction authors of the time predicted. For example:

> The Earth's population had more or less stabilized at around 9.6 billion.
>
> Relatively little colonization of other planets (in this solar system or any other) had taken place.
>
> People still lived and drove around in normal (if smaller and more energy efficient) homes and motor vehicles.
>
> We had somehow managed to avoid blowing ourselves sky-high with the assistance of nuclear weapons.

In other words, not a lot had changed (at least not nearly as much as those of earlier generations had hoped/expected). Still, what *had* changed was certainly worthy of note:

In the year 2482 CE, the United States of America elected its first woman president. She made a fine president too, doing a significantly better job of running the country than did pretty much all of the male presidents to precede her. In fact, so good of a job did she do, people were finally forced to admit that whether a president had a penis or not was something that really *did* matter after all. On the day it all began, she was about halfway into an extraordinarily successful first term.

Editorial

11.

By "it" of course I mean this particular chapter of my story.

It was about 7AM on a cool July morning over the equatorial Atlantic, cool in part because the sun had yet to fully rise, but cooler still due to the effects of global cooling. In times past, July had traditionally been one of the warmer months of the year, especially so near to the Earth's bulging waistline, where I presently sat floating with a crew of twelve others aboard the *Progenitor*, a merchant marine vessel in the service of Queen Lavinia XXX of Holland.

As we made our way north along the eastern coast of South America, our vessel's solar powered engines propelling us along at a rate that would surprise most readers, I stood shivering on deck in my thermal pyjamas, thinking to myself that either there was another ice age coming, or there simply wasn't a *trace* of carbon left in the atmosphere to trap any of the sun's energy where we needed it most – on our freezing, goose-pimpled hides.

So effective had the advent of widespread "clean" energy been in reducing all levels of heat trapping gases, the polar ice caps had actually *grown* substantially over the last five centuries, reaching approximately 20 degrees further north and 30 degrees further south than they did in times our reader is more familiar with. Nome, Alaska had been completely buried beneath the resulting sheet of expanding glacier, and a new canal had to be cut through the ice which formed each year around the Cape of Good Hope, far to the south.

Whereas the concern five hundred years ago had been that these unfathomably vast snow caps were melting, causing the world's many coastal settlements to be inundated by the great oceans (a fear which came partially true), today it was just the opposite – so much extra water had been frozen at the colder extremes of the planet that the sealine had actually *dropped* by nearly two thousand feet! When the lost city of Atlantis was finally discovered a mere 30 miles off the original coast of Crete, everyone wondered how we ever could've lost track of it in the first place…

But while many were happy to have reclaimed so much land from Neptune's briny grasp, for mariners such as I it was a complete disaster. New harbors could not be constructed fast enough to replace their landlocked predecessors. And as if this weren't bad enough, those of us who lived on/made our living from the world's waterways lost a substantial percentage of real estate/market share in the process.

Editorial

As I stood on the deck that frigid July dawn, surveying the dense stretch of wind power turbines planted in the miles of muck that used to be the bay of Brasilia, I thought to myself what a welcome sight a towering brown smokestack, belching forth great noxious clouds of grey smoke, would have been just then.

It was around nightfall by the time we reached what was left of the Gulf of Mexico. As we were well ahead of schedule and in no particular hurry to deliver our cargo of Danish Jambalaya to *New* New Orleans (Old New Orleans being too far inland to be reached by ship), we decided to drop anchor a few hundred miles south of our port of call, breaking out a few cases of soy beer and celebrating just for the sake of it before crawling into our levitating hookless hammocks for the night.

12.

We were awakened by a seismic vibration like nothing I'd experienced since the great tsunami that took place off the coast of Sri Lanka, almost half an era ago. So deep was the rumbling of the ocean, so shrill were the shrieks from the tortuous metal hull of our ship, that even the air in which our hammocks hung seemed to grind, rend, and split. A sea of dead yellow, red, and brown faces flashed across the insides of my tightly closed eyelids, and before the emergency lights began to flicker on and the siren began to wail, I thought that perhaps I'd finally crossed over to greet them.

On deck it was absolute madness, each of us dozen sailors trying in vain to understand what had just happened and what we were now seeing.

To the north and south, a rim of red fire streaked across both horizons, bright enough to rival the intensity of Sol rising from the east or retiring to the west, magnified and reflected in every direction by a perfect mirror of ocean. Yet this couldn't be the sun, we reasoned, for so black was the night sky (or what remained of it in the strip of darkness above) that the fire only seemed to burn higher and brighter than would've been possible in even the most extreme of atmospheric illusions... It was most assuredly before dawn, and yet here was what could only be the advent of a great glaring star in the two *least* likely places simultaneously, each ominous ray refracted exponentially in the seismic ripples now spreading across the water. One could not look directly at this fantastic spectacle for too long without bringing oneself near to the point of blindness.

We checked, double checked, and triple checked (God *knows* how many times we checked!) our instruments meticulously, as if a mere mix up the cardinal points would be enough to explain the sudden appearance of two blazing suns from two opposite directions (not even the correct directions) at 2:38 in the morning.

So bright was the fire both behind and before us that only a thin halo of night was left visible in the sky directly above the equator, its puny speckling of stars, once so brilliant against their backdrop of black velvet, growing ever dimmer in comparison as we sailed out of one inferno and into another.

I had been a sailor for many years; never had this been more true of any man or woman, save perhaps for Orlando, the greatest and most intrepid of all hermaphrodites. Yet in all those centuries and millennia of traversing the waters of the globe – from Lisbon to Lesbos and everything else beyond and in between – never before had I seen anything the likes of which I was seeing now.

"Well Mateys" I say, glancing at their red, blistering faces all around me, "we'd better get a move on…"

13.

Within a few hours the true sun rose from the east and began making its way along the equatorial corridor set up for it between the twin glares hemming it in from both sides. The further north of the equator we sailed, the harder it was to tell where the light was coming from. But soon enough the sea itself began to seem as red as the sky, having nothing else to reflect, and the sun – like a hot coal passing down between the ruddy walls of the esophagus – eventually completed its passage over the western horizon and into the great stomach of the Earth.

I could only suppose that if the west represented the stomach, then east must have been the mouth, and somewhere between them on the other side of the world (probably closer than we thought) was undoubtedly the anus. Yet set as the sun might, no darkness did us overtake… And while the fires to the north and south continued to burn as brilliantly as ever, something even queerer had become apparent to our senses:

We'd been sailing north for nearly an entire day, but somehow we'd yet to spy land…

Even if we'd been sailing to New Orleans, on the Gulf's original shore (nearly 150 kilometers further north from *New* New Orleans), we would've been there hours ago already. If our instruments were still functioning correctly, and they gave no indication that they weren't, we had already overshot our destination by over 375 kilometers, which would've put us somewhere in the middle of Arkansas – an impossibility in any case, since this was even *further* inland.

Still, we had larger concerns at the moment than merely being lost. It wasn't long before our protracted exposure to the red luminescence (short wave radiation?) began to have an adverse effect on the crew's health. In fact I'm sure that most of them would've jumped ship by now, if any of them had any idea where we actually were (and if the sea weren't actually boiling all around us). By now the lot of them were staggering around in various states of doneness, their initial heat blisters having given way to skin, flesh, and organs that had been cooked perfectly to order.

The well done crewmembers were already strewn about the deck, blackened on the outside and nearly devoid of all juices on the inside, their empty eye sockets staring up at the cruel red chef of their undoing. The medium fellows stood none too far behind, each of them in various phases of what could only be radiation sickness, puking and shitting and spontaneous bursting into flames here and there as they dropped to join their more fortunate brethren already on the deck. And then there were those merely rare, still in possession of their basic functions and even a vague hope of survival, somehow – their insides yet uncooked – mumbling theories on our present predicament and half-heartedly suggesting more positive scenarios, all the while as their toes, fingers, and genitals blackened and fell from their bodies like rotten fruit from withered vines.

Editorial

And then there was me – soft, supple, and pink as the day I'd shed my first skin.

Sometime, somewhere in the not-too-faraway distance, a small black book was closing…

14.

I forget how long we drifted there in that endless deadness of sea. Though the radiation affected me much less so than my fellow shipmates, lying now in disheveled piles of fossilized flesh and faintly glowing bones, my brain had been somewhat addled by the combined shocks of the last few days/weeks/months, and needless to say (though I'll say it anyway) I was having a hard time functioning.

For all intents and purposes I was just as dead as the rest, my near-static hulk seeming to spread further and further out from my center of being, blanketing and intermingling with the still-active energies of the more distinct forms representing Ishmael, Billy Budd, Admiral Nelson and all the rest.

I had begun to suspect that I was about to undergo another transformation when I felt my spirit begin to consolidate and seize upon a new, as yet unnoticed stimulus in my environment. The sky, which had seemed to blaze every conceivable shade of red, orange, and yellow from horizon to horizon only moments ago, was now nearly devoid of color entirely, save for the dark, greenish grey that blotted out whatever was left behind it, and reduced the smoldering embers on our stern and bow to the gentlest hues of pink.

And I was very warm.

In fact, I had never felt hotter in over a thousand years. And it was only growing hotter the further northwest (how could I know?) we drifted. Something truly strange and unprecedented was surely afoot, certainly stranger than Aurora Borealis, Fata Morgana, or even the Flying Dutchman... And as I lay there on the sizzling deck, my immortal skin feeling all of the pain and yet refusing to accept its attendant damage, I doubted that our ship's instruments would be of very much use now – even if they hadn't already melted and burned away completely.

I had begun to dematerialize yet again when the *CRASH* of the hull against what could only have been land shocked me back into a form more corporeal. My consciousness, having spilled out across the red hot metal of the deck, had been steadily dripping into the ocean only moments ago. Now, rescinding its long psychic tendrils – like ghostly jellyfish in our wake – it commanded my body to its feet, its eyelids to open, and its pupils to dilate to the point where, reflected in their black oily pits and the amorphous nerve centers within, the following imagery came into focus:

A long, low range of bald, capless mountains, black against the lingering red on the horizon as they wound their way off into the distance. A sea like stagnant blood beneath the heavy, oppressive shadow of the leaden, greyish green atmosphere above. And in the foreground, a barren atoll, atop which sat a peach pink, medium-sized house of the style one often saw in ancient history books.

Editorial

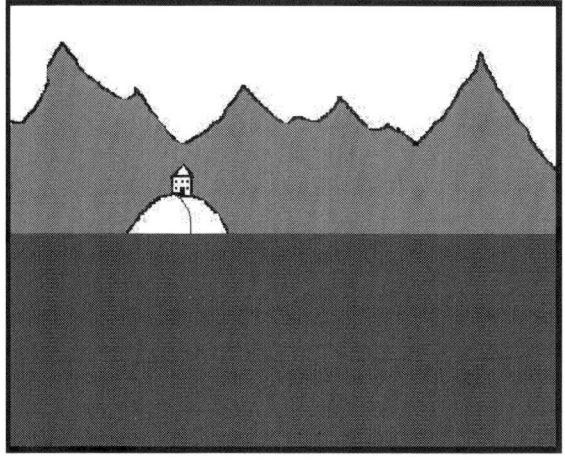

I was reasonably sure that, beneath the rosy pink of this dawning new era, the house was just as drab and grey as I'd once remembered it.

15.

The vile scribbling hordes from the godless lands of page 33 have finally breeched the defenses of page 34, overrunning and defiling its virgin white fields forevermore. The rear guard (having left most of the heavy fighting to those on the frontlines) nevertheless continue to crowd and push across the remaining territories of the conquered land, vying for their place in line amongst the dwindling scraps…

And then – a resounding thud as the imitation leather-bound covers meet, and their contents are returned to their hiding place beneath the editor's desk.

16.

Meanwhile, a man in a ragged blue jacket was making his way down the coast, turning inland toward Reno, when a call came in from Vancouver – Return to HQ immediately; urgent business. Some trouble with a new agent, no doubt.

The third person, recognizing their redundancy, takes to the backseat where they belong. You, acknowledging your utter lack of utility, quietly fall asleep on the passenger side. And I…

I say, who would have to clean up his mess? *Me*, of course. It seems that whenever one of the West coast greenhorns takes a royal shit while on the job, it is *I* that they invariably send in, with my wires and brushes and whatnot, to clean up and unclog the whole foul mess. In the end (does it end?), it will be *I* to take up their missed orders, give their missed demonstrations, and make their missed deliveries. Shit, they've got me holding hands with these pricks so tightly, *I* might as well be making their courtesy calls for them on top of it…

Silhouettes of cacti race across my windshield as the tumbleweeds struggle to keep pace with the spinning of my tires. I had nearly crushed the damned steering wheel to dust in my grip and ground my teeth down to enamel powder before I realized just how tightly I was

Editorial

wound. With the speedometer needle buried as far as it could go into the right side of the dash, I was like a coiled snake in the moment before the strike.

On my way into the Oasis parking lot I managed to lay down quite a strip of rubber before coming to a screeching stop, just barely, in my usual spot out front. I got out of the station wagon with a flourish and slammed the door extra hard. It was then that I noticed the sizable bulge protruding from the front of my pants. Somehow I'd managed to channel all of my mounting tension into an aching erection, and it was as if my penis had now become the snake, muscular and deadly (such were the delusions I commonly entertained). I tucked it into my belt as best I could, which wasn't very well.

I knew just what I needed to get straight (or unstraight, rather) and I knew just where to find it…

Throwing open the diner's glass double doors in what must've looked like quite a grand gesture, I made a scan of the occupants inside, deliberately passing over the unsavory mélange of waitresses and truckers while taking a detailed survey of the various working girls on duty that day. Too fat. Too skinny. Too pretty (too expensive). Too ugly. Now *here's* one…

Seated in a far corner by herself was all the woman I'd need. She perceived as much immediately as I crossed the room to meet her, slowly blinking her cold, golden eyes, crossing and uncrossing the length of luscious leg that disappeared into the darkness beneath her yellow and brown polka dot miniskirt. A matching snakeskin purse sat in the booth beside her.

"Can I buy you something to eat?" I asked (*this was the code at this particular truck stop, among many others*).

"Sure honey," she replied, "I'll take two eggs, uncracked and uncooked," pausing before adding "and some nice raw sausage too, if you can afford it."

An ambiguous gleam shone in the center of her oddly shaped, almost vertical pupils. This obviously wasn't her first day working the Johns at the Oasis, I thought. Wonder why I'd never seen her there before...

Without negotiating the specific terms of the deal or stalling any further, I took her by the hand and led her, slinking, out the side door and in the direction of the motel on the other end of the lot, where I planned to rent a room in which to "feed" her in private. We were almost halfway there when I involuntarily began to veer off to right, almost as if to turn around and head back in the other direction. It was then that I noticed the slightest resistance, so slight that I hadn't even realized that it was SHE now who was leading ME (all along?) – my powerful hand hopelessly ensnared in her long, surprisingly strong fingers.

"Back here" she directed, flatly, leading me back around the corner of the diner's rear. Stopping along a section of wall between a stack of old windowpanes and an exposed pile of rusty engine parts, she knelt down before me and began to unbuckle my belt and trousers. Despite my growing apprehension, I was still just as hard as ever. When I realized what was about to happen, I felt a sudden urge of panicked excitement.

"Are you sure this is safe?" I asked her, knowing full well that it wasn't, glancing about nervously at the vast expanses of desert all around us.

"Don't worry baby..." she said, or seemed to hiss, fishing out the eggs and giving them a preparatory flick of her strangely forked tongue, *"the outdoorsssssss getssssss me sssssso HOT..."*

17.

As she sucked the eggs I could feel their contents about to be drained at any moment, but I was too distracted by another sensation to allow them to crack just yet. It was as if my entire body was slowly being taken down by the peristaltic muscles of her throat. With my eyes so far in back of my head out of near agonizing ecstasy, it was as if I could literally see my insides, dark and red, becoming one with her own.

When at last she released her grip, I was able to see again for a moment as she hiked her yellow and brown polka dot dress up around her hips and prepared for the second course. With my back against the wall and her bent over in front of me, I watched with great interest as my meat sank between her posterior set of lips, passing in and out through the gentle rocking motion which she so generously provided (for I could not move myself). As her thrust became more and more violent, my eyes began to lose their function once again, only this time from the awful pressure behind them! Try as they may to retreat back into the twin recesses of my skull, it was simply no use. Besides, there was something *else* that was forcing them outward upon the world as well…

Through rapidly failing vision I could faintly discern some sort of rash spreading across her buttocks and the small of her back, scaly yellow and brown patches of skin in the glare of the red sun afternoon.

Must be the aridity of the place I thought, vaguely, as the shadows of cacti grew long.

In any event, there was nothing I could do at this point but allow her to finish me off. A sidelong glance at our obscured reflection in the dirty stack of windowpanes confirmed as much; so conjoined had we become in our entanglement, it was hard to tell whether she was still coiled around me or whether I had disappeared inside of her altogether – an odd bulge here, a stirring within there, the suggestion of a human face imprinted on reptilian hide... Only my testicles could be positively identified, tiny and protruding from some great unidentifiable orifice. At this point the meager meal of eggs and sausage seemed a mere appetizer to a royal banquet, of even less consequence than they had been before.

With one final gulp and a pop of relocating jaws, the yellow and brown scaled snake – augmented now by a slight blue iridescence – slithered slowly out into the sands heading east, periodically giving a dry, contented belch as it hauled its sated bulk in the direction of Washington DC, dragging a new pair of pink, shiny balls behind it.

18.

When the quaking finally subsided, everyone in the Oval Office, from the lowly press secretary to the nation's top general, was huddled in the corner beneath Reagan's bust. The smell of excrement was heavy in the air.

Only one person remained standing, more or less in the same position she had occupied before the bombs fell – the woman in the greenish grey suit (or, more specifically, the President of the United States).

Editorial

"Has there been an attack?" squealed the press secretary, trying in vain to conceal the large, dark wet spot which was rapidly spreading from his crotch.

"*OH GOD OH GOD OH GOD*" moaned the general, clutching the seat of his pants.

"Are we under attack?"

The president made no reply, gazing out the window behind her desk, flicking her tongue disdainfully as she focused her attention on the bright red glows now emanating from both the north and the south.

"The commies finally did it!" came the anonymous assertion from the back of the huddle. "New York and Cape Canaveral are both TOAST!!!"

"No such luck" countered the president sharply, her eyes narrowing vertically as she finally succeeded in averting her gaze, but not so much her mind, from the antipodal clouds of red nuclear gloaming on the horizon.

"Everyone to the ark."

19.

Originally constructed during the Cold War (which was actually quite heated, to be honest), *Ark Force One* was a massive vessel built to withstand whatever the sea or anything else could throw at it. Large enough to accommodate all ranking White House staff and their favorite families/mistresses/lobbyists, stored in a secret underground harbor accessible directly from the Oval Office via an equally secret high-speed rail system, it would serve as the administration's lifeline in the event of high level disaster.

Somehow, not one United States president had ever found use for it – not in the nation's entire history of nonstop war.

Maybe that had something to do with the fact that every nuclear war fought up to that point (there'd been several) had been fought on dry land. Now that land was getting scarcer by the second, as a result of the first nuclear war on ice, the boat would finally see its maiden voyage!

By the time the president and four score other passengers reached the gangplank, the sea level was already reaching the point where they'd be lucky to escape through the already dangerously narrow cave entrance. Luckily, the engineers had been notified to have the ark ready to set sail well in advance of their arrival, and were able to negotiate the ship through its rapidly closing jaws before the sea swallowed them forever. Somehow, they made it.

Well, all but their satellite navigation system …

Editorial

Without so much as a sextant to guide them and the radio fried by a massive electromagnetic pulse, produced by the thousands of nuclear warheads let loose across the Arctic and Antarctic ice sheets, the president and her administration were in for one long, lonely ride. Shielded from the lethal levels of radiation outside by a triple-thick hull of lead, the ark's occupants were able to safely view the reddening of the sea and sky, between which they were sandwiched, through the vessel's numerous periscopes. The excitement was palpable, the president thought – and thoroughly appetizing…

20.

Twenty-eight minutes after the first bombs blew, setting off a chain reaction that melted both polar ice caps almost instantly, the entire east coast of North America had already vanished completely beneath the waves. New York and Cape Canaveral were still there, of course, right along with DC and every other coastal city in the world, though not in any way that their recently drowned citizens (or anyone without a good submarine) could readily appreciate.

Soon, everyone and everything below the highest elevations would share the same fate. But that's what happens when such an astounding measure of fresh water (7 million trillion gallon to be exact), previously stored frozen at the top and bottom of the globe, is spontaneously released into the (seemingly) bottomless ocean. Well, as it turned out, whether the ocean was truly bottomless or not, it was certainly far from topless. And this was what the people of the world, if they learned anything in their short, ignorant lives, learned on that day.

The polar ice caps had melted – this much was clear to anyone who wasn't a member of a Mormon fundamentalist cult (who were more inclined to believe that the flood came from the celestial tears of the prophet himself). The other 99.999% of the world's population (the few still alive anyway) were also in agreement on another matter: the *cause* of the spontaneous melting.

It was no secret that the more powerful nations of the world had been using the poles to store their excess nuclear arms since the *Not-In-My-Backyard Treaty* of 2212 (at which the Earth's Eskimo population was notably underrepresented). Some of these munitions had obviously been detonated in the Arctic and Antarctic regions, thus triggering the explosion of the many other nuclear bombs which had been stored beneath the ice. With as many nukes squirreled away up there and down there as there were, no one was particularly surprised when both places went the way of the proverbial snowball in Hell.

What remained a mystery was *why* the bombs went off in the first place. With over half the world's population currently underwater, four fifths burnt to ashes on land, and a scant one tenth protected in bunkers underground, sealed away in some other sanctuary, or miraculously high enough above it all to survive the immediate fallout, there simply weren't that many people left to ask – and even fewer who could be counted upon to give a reliable answer.

The various theories were quite predictable.

Editorial

The Muslims blamed the Jews. The Jews blamed the Muslims. The poor blamed the rich. The rich blamed the poor. The United States (what remained of it anyway) blamed everyone but itself.

But then again, no nation or group of people can be thought of as sharing such a monolith of opinion. There was at least one US citizen, for instance, who refused to believe that the catastrophe had been the work of gay communist Nazis. She refused to believe this because (among other logical reasons) she knew fully well who had engineered the entire thing. From the moment she'd picked up the first tremors from the explosions taking place thousands of miles away (and the earthquakes and tsunamis set off around the world moments later), the president knew *exactly* who had chosen to set them off, and why they chose to do so.

21.

For hundreds of years already, the Nation of International Conglomerates (NINC), along with their partners in the traditional nation states, had been pushing for population control legislation and whipping up paranoid fears of a coming resource war – this despite the fact that world's governments had, by and large, learned to cease their destructive conflicts by this point in history and actually *share* what the combined efforts of nature and technology could provide for the global population.

So why would anyone seek to undo such a balance, destroying the closest thing to utopia mankind had ever accomplished?

Well, the simple fact was that world peace and cooperation (and the welfare system it entailed) was simply not profitable, at least not to those few who felt entitled to profit more, far more, than everyone else. From the perspective of the NINC – still by far the richest group of individuals on the planet – the social and political trajectory of the last few centuries (culminating in, among other horrors, the election of a WOMAN to the presidency of the United States) had done irreparable harm to their carefully accumulated intergenerational wealth. And while they knew that they would never again enjoy quite the lifestyle of privilege enjoyed by their great, great, great, great grandsires, they were determined to take what steps they could toward reducing this great injustice levied upon them by the ungrateful masses of the world.

The intelligent reader is surely wondering at this point how flooding all but 5% of the planet's inhabitable land (and making what was left largely uninhabitable as well) could possibly have been in the best interest of the NINC. Didn't the corporate state by its very nature NEED poor people, *lots* of poor people, in order to turn the wheels of its great profit-producing machines? Well, yes – once upon a time. In *these* times, the times in question – a time by which the proletariat had made major gains at the minor expense of the bourgeoisie – the masses of the world constituted nothing short of a massive DRAG on the coffers of the wealthy, who early in human history had become quite accustomed to having everything given to them for nothing. No longer did their former slaves work the long, grinding hours which produced so many long, leisurely hours for them. No longer did they line up to buy the expensive fruits of their own cheap labor. Rather, they enjoyed expansive periods throughout the day and night when they didn't have to work for someone

Editorial

else in order to survive (imagine that!). Needless to say, the NINC didn't like that one bit. And it was on this basis that they decided to take action.

22.

Their thinking went something like this:

The poor, for all of their utility in producing our goods and services throughout time, are at this advanced stage in human history both producing and purchasing far less than they ever have before. The social and political climate of the time gives them free access to all of the food, clothing, medicine, housing, and other basic necessities they need to live. This in turn allows them to spend less time working and more time with their families, neither of which is profitable to us and both of which have actually put quite a sizeable dent in our profits as of late – a rather disturbing trend that shows no signs of waning. Therefore, as they are no longer useful to us, and are in fact becoming more and more of a pain with each passing act of populist legislation, we have decided that it is in our best interest to simply get rid of them.

In order to accomplish this goal, we shall take advantage of the current interna-

tional tendency to consolidate nuclear munitions at the planet's poles and detonate these all at once. This course of action will carry the distinct advantage of drowning and burning to death all who cannot afford to protect themselves from the great explosion's devastating effects, while those who can afford to do so will be well-protected in specially designed underground vaults. We, of course (the NINC), will decide where to build these havens and who to sell them to. These we will draw primarily from our allies in business and government and select others we deem worthy of taking part in this bold reshaping of the world. They and theirs will be kept safe and comfortable in an enclave of their choosing until the time comes for them to emerge from this period of stasis and begin the work of helping us rebuild human society, to the level of greatness it was once destined, as both our friends and our servants. By our most generous estimates, the ensuing fallout should be reduced to safe levels and the sun will shine again within 300-500 years.

No time at all when one is kept preserved AND entertained all at once in one of our patented Holodecs (currently in the final phases of development), which will not only prevent our clients from aging and wasting away, through the use of hyperbolic seals and electric muscle stimula-

tion, but will also provide them with enough preprogrammed sitcoms, reality television shows, and pornographic videos to keep them blissfully unaware of all else until a time when they absolutely can no longer afford to.

As for our own needs, we should be able to convert our existing facilities (giving those in coastal regions particular priority) into water-tight, gamma-proof compounds at a reasonable overhead. Even where our investments in triple-thick lead coatings, state of the art life support systems and the like run far over budget, we should have little cause for concern, as it will not be long before all the world's currencies are rendered completely and utterly worthless. In the coming age, the only thing of value will be the implements enabling human life, a market in which the NINC shall hold an unbreakable monopoly.

Investing in the future has never been so free of risk. What a wonderful feeling this is.

Somewhere relatively close in the space-time continuum, yet inconceivably far away in terms the reader would understand, a book was opening – a small, black, imitation leather-bound book, of the variety sold in department stores around the world, is *opening…*

23.

The president's ark is presently gliding unguided toward a small atoll in the middle of what used to be New Mexico, or Nebraska. There is only one survivor onboard this vessel, that survivor being the president herself, who by now is used to being the only one surviving in situations like this. The rest of the passengers, having finally ceased their function as presidential sycophants and taken on the more important function of presidential sustenance, are all now either in the process of working their way through her long, tubular body, or else making way for that body as it glides through their dust which was once her shit.

The rank odor of the reptile house, simultaneously dank and dry, is thick within the cabin.

Leaving serpentine ripples in its wake across the dead, blood-black morass which now encompassed 95% of the earth's surface, the radio-less, satellite-less ark, as if guided by heat-seeking pits in its bow, was now fast approaching its prey. Having nearly wound a circle around both the world and itself by now, creating a new meridian for a new era, the snake's *rattle* suddenly came into view on the distant horizon, its hard yet flexible body like a calcified scrotum containing nothing more than two tiny, shriveled nuts.

The snake must be FED!!!

Jaws unhinged and ready to swallow the scrotalesque rattle along with the rest of the atoll it had run aground upon, *Ark Force One* comes to a thunderous crashing halt in the backyard of none other than aunt and uncle's house.

A dazed young man in the ragged remnants of a sailor suit staggers to his feet on the deck of the *Progenitor*, while the hermetic seals on the entrance to the great leviathan before it pop off one by one in rapid succession, finally releasing the hatch to reveal a tall, sinuous woman in executive attire. Their gazes meet and soon they are disembarking their respective vessels, slowly making their way down a series of chutes and ladders and gangplanks and into the barren yard of the house, never breaking eye contact as their paths patiently converge (all the time in the world) on the miraculously intact front porch, still sagging as low as ever, yet refusing to cave in completely, even after so many centuries of neglect.

Perhaps it was the neglect which *sustained* it?

Joining hands as the sky began to clear and the ships rusted down to less than nothing, the man and the woman on the porch stepped through the front door of the house in the shadow of the great jaws closing around the rattle, a covenant complete – the world reborn.

Arthur Graham

Editorial

II

24.

The elevator is crowded as the editor boards it at the 14th floor. The first thing he notices, after the thoroughly unpleasant sensation of being in such close proximity to so many people, with their sheer loathsome presence, is the strange quality of the light.

It was much brighter in the elevator, he decided, brighter than when he had last used it that morning and brighter still than he could ever remember it being. He squints his eyes to shield them from the blinding rays.

Trying his best to avoid eye contact with the elevator's other passengers, he still cannot resist the temptation to examine their faces on the periphery of his vision, safely reflected through the intermediary of the polished mirrored doors. They are squinting too, all 6 of them – 4 men, 2 women – such is the intensity of the light shining down from above.

Bodies begin to fidget and throats begin to clear, and suddenly the dirt beneath their fingernails and the scuffs upon their shoes become the most fascinating things ever witnessed. But they have only just cleared the 9th floor on their way down to the 1st and the charade is already beginning to wear thin.

The elevator continues to fall at a feather's pace and the people inside are becoming rather nervous. If they do not find some excuse to acknowledge one another, some sort of common ground on which to build a conversation, then the ride to the ground floor will surely last an eternity and they will all be forced to endure innumerable psychic deaths in the process.

Then it suddenly occurs to one bright (brightly lit) individual to bring up the one thing on their collective mind. Turning to the woman beside him, he seems to squint his eyes extra hard as he prepares to speak.

Don't do it; don't do it you sonofabitch…

The man appears to falter for a moment, but it is already too late for him to stop – once certain wheels get to turning in people's heads, it is damn near impossible to put them in reverse.

Don't do it you fool! The obvious will kill you all PHYSICALLY!!!

The lights begin to flicker, and the man's twisted face begins to speak.

"Sure is bright in…"

Before he can finish his sentence (which the reader can safely do for themselves), the lights go out altogether. When they come back up, all but the editor are lying dead on the floor, their once painfully squinted eyes now completely bugging out of their skulls.

Editorial

Carefully stepping over the great tangle of limbs and torsos before him, the editor leaves the elevator at the main lobby, clutching a small, black, imitation leather book closely to his chest as he makes for the exit.

He bumps into an old woman on the street as he hurries through the building's revolving doors, stepping on a snail as he corrects his trajectory.

CRUNCH

He then notices that the entire sidewalk is covered in snails, literally millions of them – some alive, most dead – each of them lying about in various stages of demolition, the houses they grew up in reduced to irreparable wrecks by a single careless, callous step. The amalgam of slime and shattered shell, now several inches deep at points, begins to take on the texture and appearance of the concrete itself. The editor is running.

CRUNCH
CRUNCH
CRUNCH
CRUNCH
CRANCH
CRANCH
CLAMP
CLAP

Suddenly he freezes in his snail-strewn tracks. He must go back for his book! It was in his hands only a moment ago, but now it is no longer in his hands. Where could it have gone? The old woman – really a rival editor with his own aspirations to become a writer, only this editor is too well paid, and hence has no time or motivation to write a great novel of his own... Instead, he goes about stealing the work of *others* and selling it to *his* publisher! How could our editor have been such a fool? From halfway down the block now, he can see right through the thief's cheap old woman disguise. He reverses his course and begins to give chase.

> *CLAP*
> *CLAP*
> *CLAP*
> *CLAP*
> *CLAP CLAP CLAP*
> *CLAP CLAP CLAP CLAP CLAP*
> *CLAP CLAP CLAP CLAP CLAP CLAP CLAP*

The editor cannot seem to catch up with his rival and the book they've stolen no matter how fast he runs, because he is now in the middle of a crowded assembly hall, applauding despite himself as he automatically takes part in a standing ovation for the book he's just written, the book now held in the hands of the smug, smiling man in tuxedo onstage – the rival editor!

The editor onstage seems to look directly at the editor in the audience as he launches into his thoroughly pretentious and completely insincere discussion of what the book means to him, his readers, and the world at large (this of course followed by the obligatory list of wholly undeserved thank yous).

> "First of all I would like to thank my wife…"

What kind of woman could possibly stay married to this sleaze? I had a wife myself, once…

Editorial

"...and of course I can't forget to thank my publisher..."

And who in their right mind would publish this kind of trash? I'd seen better prose scrawled on little yellow notes tucked behind toilet paper dispensers in men's public restrooms...

"...and last but not least, I would like to thank God for making this all happen."

God?
God.
GOD!?!?!

At this our editor can no longer control himself. He flings his raging form forth from his seat, nearly tearing off the armrests and knocking the heads off of those seated in front of him, literally frothing at the mouth as he makes a wild leap for the stage screaming:

"GOD? I *am* GOD you sorry sonofabitch!!!"

He is restrained with some effort by security and taken in for evaluation and overnight observation at the local mental health clinic. By early the next morning, the doctors are able to determine the cause of his demented outburst:

Ink poisoning.

Several hours more and they've finally managed to extract the last of the pen fragments, paper wads, and pieces of black, imitation leather from out of his stomach and the topmost portion of his small intestine.

25.

The year is 3117 CE. No one reads books anymore, because all of the books have been destroyed by an exotic wood pulp eating virus. Along with destroying all of the books already printed, it has also destroyed most of the trees previously utilized in their printing.

When human civilization (not *quite* bombed all the way back to the Stone Age, but close) attempted to resurrect earlier forms of paper and print making, they found that papyrus, parchment, and everything else they tried to make books from succumbed to the virus as well. There was just no use at all – no sooner than they'd reissue what fragments of their once vast body of collective literature that could be recalled, or endeavor to create new compositions for the new world, the virus would mutate and whatever these words were printed on was soon reduced to dust as well.

Editorial

It was postulated by some that it was the ink which carried the virus, or else somehow invited its deleterious effects. But despite the many different experiments with various ink/paper combinations, whatever compositions they managed to complete, even those specially preserved in lead and copper pyramids (another rediscovered technology) lasted only marginally longer than previous attempts. In the end it hardly seemed worth the effort, especially when there were so many meals to be hunted and gathered, so many mutant abominations to do battle with... Reduced to conditions even harsher than those faced by their ancestors (who never had to contend with saber-toothed sureties salesmen), mankind as a whole found even less use for reading than it had in the final centuries before the collapse.

At least this time they had a good excuse.

Of course, there was no use trying to read books in electronic format either. The great satellites and relay stations that had once formed the nodes and pathways of the "world wide web" were now nothing more than oversized tin cans in Earth's orbit, and every laptop desktop and palmtop had had its brains fried in a similar fashion – rendering them much more useful for barricading doors or smashing over the heads of enemies and prey than for reading electronic books. They were probably always better suited to these sorts of uses in the first place, given the level of comprehension possessed by some of the people who had once used them...

And the fact remained that not many people wanted to read anyway. There had been a time just prior to the collapse, when a very small class of people had achieved a level of affluence which allowed them to pursue a variety of leisure time activities, and one of those pastimes had been reading. But then, just as now, the majority of the Earth's inhabitants had precious little time to spend putting extraneous information gleaned from books into their heads when it was hard enough just to find enough food to fill their stomachs. As for the well-fed people who still couldn't be troubled to pick up a book (at least a book that wasn't about vampires, celebrities, chicken soup, or some other nonsense) – this was a mystery that perhaps will never be solved.

But the year is 3117 CE and there are no more books – none.

Of course, this is a bold-faced lie. The very fact that the reader is reading this book now should be enough to give that away. Obviously, paper products are still very much alive and well. After all, it is not as if people had rediscovered synthetics yet (not at the time of this writing, not if it is 3117 CE and there are no more books). And they certainly weren't going to waste good hides on scribbling when the nuclear winter was still far from over. Could you imagine? Wrapping yourself in a copy of *The Wasteland*, or *The Faerie Queen*, as you prepare to leave the precious warmth of your enclosure on your way out for a midnight piss?

But how, then, was this manuscript composed? Can we accept the author's assertion, now, that paper never DID go the way of the dinosaur? After he tricked us into believing that it HAD, initially? There goes a dinosaur right now. That proves that the author is telling the truth.

Or does it?

Editorial

26.

The author/editor is now at the stake. His hands and his feet have been bound with strips of leather and his entire body is lashed tightly to the stake with hemp rope. The kindling has been placed at its base and the bonfire wood has already been stacked beneath him, all the way up to the tips of his toes. He is not expecting a favorable verdict.

"Mr. XXXXXX," intones the grand inquisitor, his crimson gold embroidered hood hanging almost as low as his voice, "you stand accused of perjury in the cosmic degree. How do you plead?"

"No contest, your honor."

"Do you wish to hear the full account of the charges against you?"

"No, your honor."

"The list is quite extensive, but nevertheless it is my duty to read it to you before judgment is passed."

Already a court peon is edging forward with his torch.

"Alright, let's hear it then…"

27.

EXHIBIT A:

There is a man in a wheelchair sitting with some friends around a campfire they've built beside an old broken down school bus. The bus is perched atop a high desert bluff of dry red earth and grey sage brush, and its windows are riddled with over 30 years worth of bullet holes. The inside of the bus is riddled with 40 years worth of rat scat. The light from the moon above and the fire below combine to cast a strange pink glow across the white hands and faces of the four friends present.

One of the friends is holding a bamboo flute to his lips, making inexpert sounds that nevertheless seem to please his drunken companions. Another friend is holding a medium-sized goat skin drum between her knees that she uses to bang out a passable rhythm. Still another friend is tinking a spoon against a beer bottle, which makes a sound like:

TINK
TINK
TINK
TINK

But there are no *tanks* that suddenly come rolling through the valley below, no steamer *trunks* that spontaneously pop open and come unpacked at the sound of this alliteration – just the sharp and unadulterated sonic exchange between the elements of quartz and silica and steel.

And then there is the man in the wheelchair, purposely sitting back away from the fire so as not to inadvertently roast his lifeless legs (a lesson he'd learned the hard way several times before), playing an Australian aboriginal pipe instrument which makes a bizarre low-pitched droning sound when one end is rubbed with beeswax and gurgled into.

The night continued with the proper amount of levity, until the music ended (but the drinks continued) and the discussion grew serious. As is inevitable under such circumstances, they eventually wound up on the subject of religion.

"Listen, man, what *really* happened was..."

The man in the wheelchair was busy explaining his theory concerning what really went down between Adam, Eve, and the serpent in the Garden of Eden. According to this revision of accepted biblical truth, Adam was a prick who never paid Eve much attention in the first place. So one day while Adam was off fucking a "goat" or whatever other animal he happened to name that day, Eve happened upon a serpent next to a tree full of rotting fruit. Since the fruit was no good anymore anyway, the serpent had decided to rest in the shade and fellate itself instead.

Eve watched with much fascination as the serpent swallowed its own tail, forming itself into a perfect circle of pleasure, and after a while she was surprised (not ashamed, for shame requires knowledge) to feel herself becoming aroused as well.

When at last the serpent came out of its ecstatic state, it noticed Eve and engaged her in polite conversation. It didn't take long for the small talk to wear thin, however, as they both knew exactly what was on each other's minds.

"I suppose you're wondering what I was doing back there, yes?"

"No, I could tell what you were doing."

"Would you like me to teach you how to do that yourself?"

"I don't know... I don't think Adam would approve..."

"Tell me, who the fuck is this 'Adam' and why should I care?"

And so Eve was instructed in the art of oral self gratification, starting with the prerequisite flexibility exercises. Being a fast learner, however (faster than Adam ever would've known), it wasn't long before she could coil herself into a ring as well, touching her tongue to the tip of her own "rattle" – licking it expertly until her whole body vibrated with the same incredible intensity.

As she lay there in the grass beside him, utterly spent and too weak to even stand, the serpent lazily slithered into position between her legs. He then collected his lesson fee according to the terms they'd discussed.

Several months and many lessons later, Adam and Eve were sitting down to dinner one night when Eve felt something stir within her. Moments later, thousands of tiny creatures came bursting forth from the crease in her loins, like serpents but with human features – some with stubby leg-like appendages, some with sporadic patches of hair, etc.

As the brood slithered and squirmed in a pile beneath her, Adam reached down and carefully picked one of them up. Holding it close to his face, studying its minute appendages, tubular body, and curious facial features (much like Eve's, he thought), his eyes suddenly lit up with idiotic glee. Holding his new discovery up to the heavens with a pride that would've shamed Satan himself, Adam triumphantly declared:

"Snake!"

There was silence around the campfire for a few moments after the man in the wheelchair finished explaining his theory. None of his friends had particularly

Editorial

enjoyed the allegory, yet *he* was in the process of laughing himself to tears. After those few moments of shock, disgust, and hysterical laughter were finally over with, one of the friends finally spoke up.

"Man, that was the most blasphemous story I have ever heard. I do believe you're going to Hell."

The other friends nodded in solemn agreement.

The man in the wheelchair, however, found the whole thing pretty easy to laugh off. After all, it was only a story! Besides, he was as drunk as a lord himself – surely the lord above would pardon his peer the heresy, he reasoned. And it wasn't as if his story were any crazier than the other versions floating around...

Drunkenly, he fumbled around on the ground beside his wheelchair, eventually producing a half empty bottle of wine, which he intended to finish before the night was over. But just as he was preparing to take a swig, a great white bolt of lightning erupted from the gathering clouds above and *ZAPPED* him right where he sat. The stench of burnt hair, skin, metal and rubber had become apparent even before the smite itself.

As the smoke began to clear and the blindness from the flash five feet before them wore off, the friends were amazed to see that the man in the wheelchair had vanished into thin air – leaving in his place little more than a man!

The man looked down in disbelief, vigorously patting his legs to dispel the chance of phantoms. He was too amazed to say much of anything else, and so he simply said:

"Well, I'll be damned..."

28.

EXHIBIT B:

Somewhere high up in the high, high Himalayas, many centuries before the Great Collapse (though it could've been many after and it wouldn't have mattered, such was their elevation), a young disciple is sitting at the feet of his wizened master on the steps of a monastery hidden carefully amongst the crags. From within its hallowed halls comes the sound of a giant gong being *GONGED*, signifying the hour at which all prayer, meditation, and other activities are temporarily interrupted for the mid-day meal.

The thick-headed disciple has been leveling question after thick-headed question at the master since

Editorial

they began their exercise several hours before. But no matter how impatient the disciple becomes in his quest for knowledge, the master is able to meet his questions in a kind and gracious (if wholly unsatisfactory) manner.

After all, this is why he is the master: He has mastered the great waiting game!

But neither one of them has eaten since the meager bowl of soy curd which was rationed out, as it is rationed out every day at the hour just before dawn, and this has imparted an obvious, if unspoken desire on both their parts to finish up with the shenanigans and hit the chow line.

"But master, you still have not answered my question!"

"That is because you have not asked a question, but an answer."

"But surely, master, you can at least give me some idea how long it will take me to reach enlightenment?"

At this the master became thoughtful, squinting his eyes and furrowing his brow in a manner which suggested true consideration. Then, after a moment, he replied:

"Oh, I'd say about ten years."

At this the disciple was incredulous.

"Ten years!" he cried, abandoning all pretense of respect, "But I don't *have* that long to wait! What if I work extra hard?"

At this the master nearly let slip the tiniest suggestion of a grin.

"Then..." he replied, looking away from the disciple and at the infinitely more interesting mountains on the horizon.

"...it will take you twenty."

The gong then *GONGED* for the second time.

29.

EXHIBIT C:

A man and a woman are seated in bed next to one another.

The woman puts aside her knitting, turns to the man and says "It sure was a wonderful day today, wasn't it honey?"

The man, upon hearing this, puts aside the gun he's been cleaning and replies "Yes honey, it surely was."

30.

And now the fires are burning, stoked to full strength now, burning hard, burning hot for all those deemed worthy of them, burning whomever fits the bill of the day, while those clever enough to dodge the check are laughing away in cooler climes (at least until their turn at the stake).

One cannot be certain from the aroma whether it is swine or human flesh that is being roasted...

Time goes by, and since time doesn't have many places to go to outside of space, and since space can be an

Editorial

awfully dull, boring place without time stirring things up, space and time team up to take care of business together. And since 100% of that business involves the building up and breaking down of all structures currently in existence, all structures not yet in existence, and all structures which can no longer be said to exist, time and space go to work sweeping up the ashes and everything else remotely associated with the editor's crimes, his trial, and execution.

And the years flow past, each one of them as unremarkable as the next, as unnoticed as nanoseconds in fact, not even long enough to contain anything notice*able* – centuries just barely registered as moments in space/time. Soon the millennia are passing by at a modest rate of 47 per minute, and of course all manner of things noticeable and not-so-noticeable occur along the way (though most of them fall in the latter category), and naturally there come periods where lying is greatly rewarded and periods where lying is greatly punished (our poor unlucky editor!), along with every other conceivable and inconceivable reversal and re-reversal of standards, and... Wait, did anyone else just hear God yawn?

It may be hard for the reader to imagine, but this relatively brief period of time also entailed long stretches where humans had been wiped clean off the chessboard altogether, almost invariably following the buildup of some self-fulfilling "end of the world" type prophecy, while all the while the world just kept on turning (this world and all others) as if nothing of import had taken place whatsoever.

Ho hum, another 67 civilizations wipe themselves out in the past hour, another 17 planets are destroyed or left otherwise uninhabitable by events avoidable and unavoidable.

Ho hum…

It is said by those who believe in fate that all things are determined ahead of time. It is said by those who believe in choice that history has not been written yet. On the surface, it would seem that these philosophies are completely at odds with one another, but nothing could in fact be further from the truth. For the only reason why everything is possible is because everything *will* eventually come to pass – at least on a long enough timeline. And since time is likely much longer than our conception of it, every possibility is bound to pan out eventually.
And yet, not a lot changes, not in this world or any other…

Ho hum.

What would be *really* exciting, now – a true first, in fact – would be if any human era managed to overcome its inherent human flaws and actually *learn* from the mistakes of its predecessors for once and EVOLVE.
But since that is probably the *least* likely thing that could ever happen, since it is much more likely that the world (and all worlds) really will end, for good some day, we can only imagine the editor's ashes being blown throughout all of space and time, carried forth by cosmic winds to fill in the tiniest cracks and crevices of the multiverse, bringing home the raw materials required for the next ultimately futile, yet ultimately necessary go-round. If it seems at all unlikely that one man could

contain enough ash for that wide of a dispersal, or that said ash could affect any kind of noticeable change on any significant scale, please keep in mind that we are talking about *the editor* here. And the only thing that an editor is capable of doing, by its very nature, is changing things (often without permission from the "original" author).

The lies of the writer are thus supplanted by the lies of the editor, which somehow results in the conveyance of truth, or a kind of it anyway…

31.

The year is 4438 CE and the vaults have yet to open. The people alive today know this to be the case because the buildings fortified by the NINC so many years ago are among the only ones of their kind left standing, sealed behind metal doors of unidentified alloys thick enough and hard enough to withstand any level of bombardment.

It is doubtful that anyone on the surface has even ever heard of the Nation of International Conglomerates, as no one claiming membership in this elitist group has ever emerged. Whether they all perished after the batteries ran out on their Holodec (patent pending) stasis chambers, leaving their mortal remains forever frozen in front of the Oprah Winfrey show, or whether they are all alive down there still, living like kings on the spoils of a world already two millennia gone, periodically checking their monitors for a reason to resurface – this is truly anyone's guess.

Perhaps they designed their barricades to be a little *too* impregnable, and the mass of them are lying in piles of bones just on the other side of these great doors as we speak. What a bunch of ninc*ompoops*!

Of course, this is just another guess. We already saw what happened to the *last* person who attempted an assertion of truth…

But the year is 4438 CE (certain as any approximation), 1,954 years following the Great Collapse. A youth of indeterminate sex is playing outside of vault J-11B, somewhere uphill from Charleston, West Virginia, pitching rocks against its door and delighting in the hard, sharp sound this makes each time. The child is nude save for a belt fashioned out of raw marl hides, from which several rudimentary instruments (could be weapons, tools) dangle.

Despite sharing the chief physical traits of its mammalian ancestors (body hair, bipedal gait, opposable thumbs), there is something distinctly reptilian about the creature. The skin seems rather scaly (or perhaps the scales seem rather skinny), the eyes are hooded with vertical pupils, and there is a rather blunt snout in the place of a proper nose. The child's lips are thin, almost nonexistent, and drawn quite tightly across its wide, expressionless mouth. It is not hard to image venomous fangs and a long, forked tongue behind them.

But, as with most things easily imagined, this was simply not the case. Were the child's mouth to suddenly open, perhaps to eat, anyone within twenty yards could see how dull its teeth were as it bit into its omnivorous fare. As its tongue protrudes to scent the air around it, anyone close enough to be detected would see how human-like (if slightly long and pointed) this organ was as well.

Editorial

Soon the child grows tired of the door, though, casting one last stone before retrieving the string of bumwots it had hunted down that afternoon from the shade of a nearby shrub. It then starts down the trail leading across the crater and back to the village on the other side. It doesn't make it very far, however, before it happens upon an adult of its tribe, sprawled out on a boulder beside the trail, basking in the day's final rays of strong sunshine.

In the tribe to which these two people belong, individuals are born with predominantly mammalian characteristics that slowly give way to more reptilian features with age. The older one gets, the scalier they become, the more time they must spend warming their blood manually, and the more their tailbones come to resemble actual tails.

This particular adult was an elder of the village at the wizened age of thirty-five.

"What's that you have there?" elder Lycix inquired feebly as young Quidan approached.

"Bumwots!" the youth informed the elder enthusiastically, taking note of its weakened state. "You look like you could use a bite, old one."

The poorly disguised hunger in Lycix's eyes had been apparent even to little Quidan.

"Care for one?"

Lycix slowly opened and closed its old, feeble mouth, making a dry smacking sound as it imagined the sweet juices of the bumwot dribbling down its parched throat.

"I haven't had a bumwot in a few day's time," replied Lycix slowly, smiling. "If you'll trade me one of yours, I won't need another for a few more."

Quidan loosened one of its kills from the marl hide belt slung low on its hips, tossing it to the elder who, despite its venerable age, managed to catch the meal with a single snap of its razor-sharp teeth. The entirety of the succulent bumwot disappeared almost instantly.

"Nothing more valuable to an old timer like me," Lycix began, belching softly, "than dinner I don't have to go chasing after myself!"

Quidan nodded solemnly at the elder's wisdom.

"Now, your payment."

Quidan's body stiffened with anticipation as Lycix slithered off its rock and onto the sand at ground level. In an exchange that had been repeated countless times since the dawn of their people's recorded history, the elder took the youth's sex gland into its mouth/put its mouth into the youth's sex gland (it wasn't clear which phase Quidan was in at the moment; could've been in between) and began the act of pleasing.

As was traditional among their people, the young and healthy provided the most physical labor (in the form of hunting and farming) and took the most sexual pleasing. For the elderly, quite naturally, things were just the opposite. And while the non-sexual needs of the tribe were usually met by the bounty of the land, there never seemed to be enough pleasing to go around, which made it a valuable commodity even in times of great material prosperity. It turned out that the aged possessed a natural surplus of it, in fact, as they had little desire for sex themselves anymore, and therefore chose to give it away in exchange for goods and services more important to them. It was quite the ideal arrangement, actually, as it gave the old and infirm a guaranteed means of subsistence, while at the same time rewarding the youth for their contributions to the greater good of society.

Editorial

When Lycix had finished, it wiped the remnants of bumwot and pleasing from its face, then languidly returned to its rock to absorb a few more hours of warmth before the sun went down in the desert. Quidan thanked the elder for the amicable trade and bade it a good evening. Lycix thanked the youth for the good deal and bade it an amicable night.

Quidan then began making its way back to the village, where its hungry mate and offspring were surely waiting. As it traipsed through the boulder field and around the corner of an ancient, massive machine, half buried in the sand, the ruins of Plimpton suddenly came into view on the far end of the crater.

Plimpton used to be a nice little town in the days before the collapse, and, had it contained a few more people of money and importance, it might've remained that way today (such was its elevation). Now, for the lack of a lead dome or any other defensive measure, its quaint, picturesque homes had been reduced to splintered black husks which would never grace another postcard, their picket fences now like hollow porcupine quills in the red desert sand.

Of course, there was no way that Quidan could've known any of this. With all but the planet's mountain lands essentially wiped clean during the great red night all those centuries ago, it was surprising that mankind (or any other kind) had managed to survive at all, let alone any of its history or culture. Certainly Quidan was at least vaguely aware that the world hadn't always been this way, and that unfamiliar others had likely come before (and would doubtless come after), but these were conclusions that any semi-intelligent creature was capable of making.

As for the DETAILS of the people who had once inhabited the bombed-out inland ruins (and the increasing number of domiciles being reclaimed from the receding waters), for all Quidan knew they had been potty trained chimps with merely passable table manners.

32.

PLIMPTON, XX, 1967 CE – Charles Duvall, known to friends (his few friends) as Charlie, or sometimes "Charlie D", was in the midst of stuffing the remainder of an undercooked bratwurst into his mustard-smeared mouth, while using his free hand to finish urinating against the wall of a downtown Plimpton alleyway. The old town clock, just visible at the top of the building around the corner, held its hands in the position indicating 1:45. The deep blue-blackness beyond it, through which its illuminated dial shone, would seem to indicate that this was after meridian.

Randomly he adjusted the belt of his pants, first sliding it one way, then back the other. When he was through, his pants and belt remained in essentially the same position.

Staggering back out into the street, the 32-year-old unemployed truck mechanic successfully stifled a succession of violent dry heaves, resisting the urge to vomit, then stumbled off in what he thought was the direction of his mother's house. It wasn't long though before he found himself once again outside of the Shelter – the Cold War themed drinking establishment from which he'd been ejected only 45 minutes before:

Editorial

"Whadaya MEAN the Unitesed STATES *hic* won Whorld Whar II maaaaaaaaaaan? Wuzza buncha German JEWS built the H-bomb ferus *hic* n' everun but US knows the commies *hic* did mosta the fightin' *hic* bof 'fore n' affer dat..."

Upon remembering this scene, during which the bartender and patrons had looked upon him with expressions of bemused disdain, Charlie was suddenly seized by an urge to smash out the building's *other* plate glass window as well. But, knowing that he'd need all his remaining energy to make it back to his childhood bed for the night, he decided against the idea and lurched off in that (he was sure this time) general direction.

The fact that he was too blind with drink at this point to even *find* a suitable brick was purely incidental.

Though it took him a few tries of wandering up and down Main, he was eventually able to locate a cross street with a name he recognized, which he followed down the hill leading out of town and into the countryside. Taking a shortcut through a field of dead, overgrown grass, he banged his shin against an old rusted fire hydrant out in the middle of it, falling to the ground and cursing it for being there, right there where he always remembered it being.

When at last he came to the wooded lane where his mother kept her small, modest home, Charlie had become so bedrowsed that he contemplated laying down in a drainage ditch on the side of the road to finish out the night. But recalling the last time he'd done that, the night that the levee broke several years previous, he thought better of the idea and spurred himself onward, dreaming of his mother's freshly laundered sheets and home cooked breakfast as he sleepwalked the last quarter mile.

Charlie fumbled with his keys, almost losing them down between the planks of the front porch as his feet, like slow-motion bullfrogs, leapt and plopped up each step and to the door. After several minutes of trying, and then minutely inspecting and trying again almost every key on his key ring, Charlie noticed the handwritten note that had been taped to the door. Squinting in the darkness, he held the note close to face so as to make out the words, which were written in his mother's handwriting:

Son –

I have changed the locks again. Your things are on the porch. Maybe one of your sisters can take you in.

Love,

- Mom

Note in hand, Charlie sat down on the porch steps and probably would've fallen asleep right there, had the flurry of thoughts inside his head subsided long enough to relax the rest of his body, through which the whole mess now flowed. In fact he was incapable of rest now, it seemed, such was his predicament. He considered banging on the door until his mother let him in, as she had at times before, but then he considered all of the other times she had not let him in, or not let him in and phoned the police as well – both of which had become increasingly frequent outcomes of late.

Editorial

And yet he couldn't bring himself to gather his few possessions and hit the road either, tethered as he was to the umbilicus of her financial support. And so with no money, no job, no productive activity to keep him occupied at all, he did what any old drunk would do and took a battered notebook out from one of the bags beside him. He'd decided to write a few notes of his own.

He began by writing a letter to his estranged wife, which he abandoned halfway through and tore up into tiny pieces, tossing them into the rose bushes beside the porch. The white speckling on the dark red and green background created a pattern resembling a blanket of stars shining through a veil of nebulous gases, but just then the sliver of moon illuminating this scene was obscured by clouds, and Charlie's attention was returned to the notebook in his hands.

Next he wrote a fictional account of his mother's sexual adventures with the animals behind several of the constellations which could be seen in the sky on clearer nights. But it was never made clear in the story whether she went up into the stars for this celestial gangbang, or whether Leo, Ursa Major and the rest descended to Earth to ravage her eager body on her own plane of existence. Still, he thought it was a pretty decent first draft regardless... These few pages he tore out of the notebook, folded neatly, and taped to the door where his mother's note had previously been.

He then jotted down a few last lines on a final sheet of paper, which he slid into an empty sandwich bag he discovered in his coat pocket. This he carefully sealed and placed back where he found it.

Feeling well enough to do so now, Charlie got up off his arse and left his mother's porch for what would be the last time. None of the bags he bothered to take. Strangely sober, he followed the dark lane back to the intersection leading into and out of town. But instead of turning left or right, he continued straight, setting off through the adjacent field and into the trees on the other end. In following this route, he knew, he would eventually come across the railroad tracks which, if followed east, would take him all the way to the disused upper harbor.

33.

Through the night he walked.

Following the tracks as they meandered through the thinning forest, on their way out to the long defunct shipyard on the once great lake, Charlie was reminded of many notable occurrences from his three plus decades in Plimpton, the town in which he'd lived his entire life. Most of these memories he'd thought long forgotten, either accidentally, like so much of a person's short existence, or else washed from his brain on purpose with the cleansing effects of alcohol.

> The time he'd lost his virginity to a bald-headed, peg-legged prostitute, right there on the railroad tracks one drunken night long ago…

> All of his other sexual encounters (most of them embarrassing failures), punctuated

by long drought seasons of celibacy and self doubt...

His first and only love, whom he had attempted to write a letter to earlier, who had (among many other endearing traits) a pussy sweet enough to swallow an entire unpeeled lemon and piss out a perfect glass of lemonade, ice cubes and all...

There were certainly remembrances of other, cleaner sorts as well, though these would likely fail to interest readers of such trash.

When at last Charlie came to the breakwall it was still quite dark out, thought it wouldn't be for much longer. In fact, the faintest traces of dawn could already be detected on the horizon as he took his first steps upon the immense concrete structure. Gentle were the small night waves lapping warmly against its cold, monolithic form. In the distance Charlie could see the lighthouse at the far end of the breakwall, its familiar silhouette gradually distinguishing itself from the hints of twilight which were now breaking through the darkness beyond. The light in the tower was out, and had been for as long as he could remember.

By the time he'd reached the halfway point, there was just enough visibility for Charlie to perceive a man holding a fishing pole, standing beside a small bucket on the edge of the platform.

Often had he encountered fishermen on the breakwall in the early morning hours, though never anywhere near this early. Then again, if there were people who got up to go fishing that early in the morning, it was not as if Charlie ever would've witnessed them anyway – he was not exactly a morning person, habitually sleeping until noon actually, which made his presence out there at this hour that much more inexplicable.

This morning, apparently, was special…

Slowly the fisherman's features materialized in the gathering gloam. He seemed to be of middle age, slim, average height. He trousers and sweater were loose and baggy, giving him the impression of being slightly larger than he as in actuality. He was bald and hatless and, at least in profile, there was something distinctly frog-like about his face.

As Charlie approached, it seemed to him more and more that the fisherman really *did* have a frog face. Perhaps it was a trick of light, or just the lack thereof that gave the fisherman this appearance, but Charlie had encountered his share of frog-like people in his life, and this person was more like a frog in the face than anyone else he'd ever chanced to meet. What was more, it wasn't just the frogman's face, but his entire *head* that seemed to have been supplanted by some monstrous, giant bullfrog.

But Charlie was neither afraid nor repulsed at all by the frogman as it turned to great him, Charlie with his coat pockets all laden with stones which he hoped would help him sink. Really, why would he be? If there could be frog-faced people in the world, and no one thought twice about accepting *them*, he reasoned, then why should he find fault with a man who literally *was* a frog from the neck up?

In any case Charlie was beginning to suspect that he was still quite intoxicated, drunk as fuck actually, which would probably make it easier for him to do what he had come out there to do, regardless of whatever hallucinations he brought along with him.

The frogman seemed to smile at Charlie's acceptance of him, signaling that the acceptance was reciprocal with a just barely registered upturn of its pale, wide mouth, and an unmistakably friendly gleam in his black, bulbous eyes. He seemed to be beckoning Charlie closer, gesturing to the contents of the bucket at his (of course) broad, webbed feet, spread out like slimy green fans across the mortar.

Peering cautiously, first at the frogman to ascertain his intent, and then into the bucket itself, Charlie's bemused curiosity immediately gave way to abject horror at what he saw: There, in the bait bucket, was a frog paddling circles – only this frog had an unmistakably *human* face and head.

And it too was smiling – directly at Charlie.

At this Charlie turned and ran as fast as his legs would carry him, faster than he had ever ran for Plimpton High (could've won that scholarship), not even slowing down to shed the coat containing his ballasts and ill-conceived suicide note. Finally, when he could at last be sure that neither the frogman nor the manfrog had given chase, he collapsed out of sheer exhaustion and fell asleep in a ditch where he would wake up several hours later, shivering in the mid-day sun.

That day Charlie withdrew most of what he had left in his bank account, bought a suit, and rented a room. A day after that, he began looking for honest work. In doing so, he managed to line up quite a few promising prospects rather quickly, much to his surprise.

Three weeks later, he received an unexpected letter in the mail. Little did he know it at the time, but his mother had decided to submit the story he'd written about her for publication. Imagine his surprise, then, when he received a check in the amount of $50 from a well-known publishing house. The check came enclosed with a note:

Dear Mr. Duvall,

We are pleased to inform you that your short story, I Loved a Lion, *has been accepted for publication in an upcoming issue. Congratulations and many best returns of the day!*

Sincerely,

XXXXXX Publishing

Charlie could barely even remember writing the story, let alone titling it so fittingly, but it hardly mattered. He placed the letter and the check on the kitchen table and finished getting ready for work, telling himself that maybe he would write another story later that evening. Though he had no way of knowing it just then, this chance occurrence would actually mark the start of a literary career that would one day prove to be quite successful.

And he never touched another drop.

Editorial

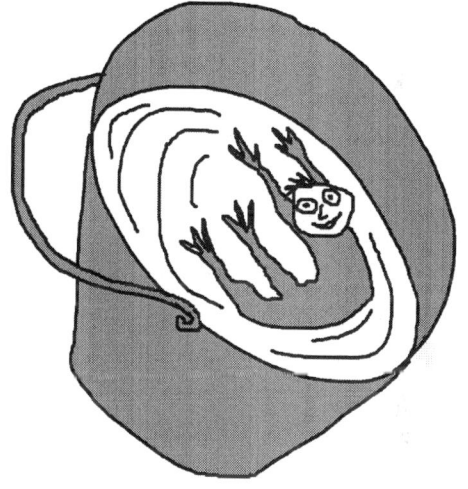

III

34.

"Let me off of this FUCKING plane I tell you I'm a FEDERAL FUCKING AGENT!!!"

The madman continued to rave in this vein despite the fact that his request was already in the process of being fulfilled (or at least trying to be fulfilled) by the flight attendant and the co-pilot as they dragged him, kicking at passengers and clawing at each seat, toward the exit at the front of the plane.

Suddenly the voice of the pilot could be heard over the speaker:

> *Ladies and gentlemen we do apologize for the delay, please rest assured that we will be taking off shortly.*

Editorial

At this the madman resumed his outbursts with twice renewed vigor.

"I AM A FEDERAL FUCKING AGENT I TELL YOU this plane is going to CRASH!!!"

A round of uneasy looks and nervous laughs swept throughout the cabin, followed by murmurs and chattering which only grew louder as the "agent" was successfully extracted from the plane and placed into the custody of airport police.

> *Once again ladies and gentlemen we do apologize for the delay...*

Then, just when the flight crew thought they'd gotten everything under control, one of the other passengers stood up, bravely defying the fasten-seatbelts sign above to address the entire cabin with a verbal parroting of their very own inner thoughts.

"Wait a minute!" he shouted, "Now hold on a sec! What if he's right? I mean, what if he's telling the *truth*?"

The uneasy looks got a little uneasier and the nervous laughter was infused with a little more nervousness as the murmurs and chattering that filled the cabin reached a near deafening pitch. The co-pilot and flight attendant wasted no time in executing the physical and verbal gestures that politely communicated SIT YOUR ASS DOWN AND SHUT YOUR MOUTH UP to everyone aboard flight 495 out of Seattle, but to no avail.

"Let me off this plane too, goddamnit!"

With no need for an escort of his own, the passenger quickly collected his things from the overhead compartment and barreled down the aisle, making a bee line for the still-open exit door without ever slowing down or looking back. The flight attendant and co-pilot were nearly knocked into opposite seats as they parted to let him pass.

To make matters worse, other passengers were starting to get ideas of their own.

> "Honey, he may be right…"
> "…I don't know, what if he is?"

Soon full-blown panic had spread throughout the cabin, and with every second that passed the flight attendant and co-pilot became less inclined to continue their efforts to quell it.

> "Suppose it's true?"
> "There's always that chance…"

Within six minutes, all 241 passengers had deboarded the plane, following each other like lemmings out onto the tarmac.

All but one asleep in the back, that is.

35.

Edward Duvall (known to the reader up until now as "the editor") woke up in the rearmost seat of the plane sometime shortly after takeoff. He was surprised, in a way, to notice that he was the only passenger. He seemed to remember the whole plane being full of people, but then again he had only had about 14 hours of sleep in the week following his book eating episode, so he couldn't be

Editorial

entirely sure that he hadn't dreamt them up. For all he knew, the lot of them had been left on the runway 10,000 feet below, left to mill about until they were run over and possibly exploded by the next plane coming in for a landing, all for the lack of someone to tell them where to go or what to do next (for the sole madman among them had been removed by airport police long ago).

In any event, the airline's policy mandating that all flights go on as scheduled, even with only one passenger onboard, meant that Edward Duvall (son of the late literary giant Charles Duvall) would soon be finding himself in Miami, Florida. For what or why he was traveling to that part of the country, that flaccid cock of the United States – just waiting for the hurricanes to subside long enough for it lay a long overdue fuck on Cuba – he was only vaguely aware.

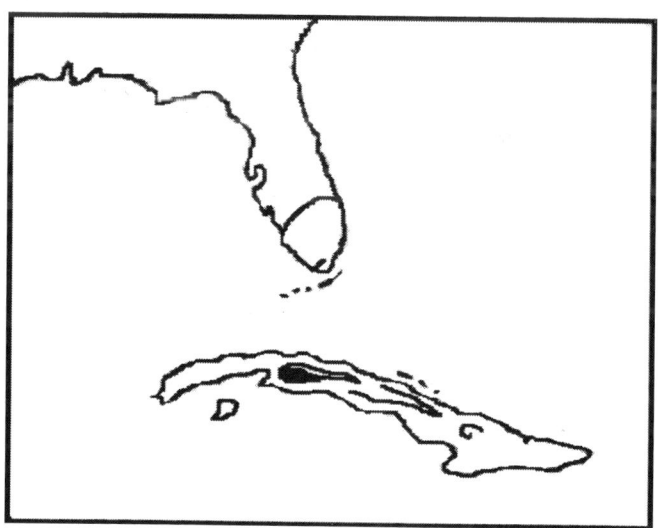

As he sat there trying to work it out, he became aware of a few other things as well – a chunk of food in his teeth, a bug in his ear, a piece of lint between his ass cheeks, irritating him greatly. And as he sat there trying to work out these other things as well, it finally dawned on him that he was traveling to Florida because he'd recently found some work in Miami.

In the end (*does* it end?), work was really the only reason why anyone went anywhere. Whether a man was hunting and killing and preparing his own food himself, or paying some other guy to do it for him, he usually found that he had to work just as hard. Sometimes Ed wondered if we'd all be better off if we started simply blowing each other in exchange for all goods and services. He wasn't entirely sure that this would necessarily entail that much less work, but either way people had to eat and probably get off at least once a day, he figured.

Needless to say (though I'll say it anyway), Ed was having a bit of a hard time focusing his thoughts on the situation at hand. As was usual for him at times like this, he began to crave and taste the sensation of alcohol upon his tongue. Back at his old job as an editor, there in the grey cubicle where he had up until recently spent most of his waking hours... Well, let's just say that the book he'd been working on – the one about the world snake and the shapeshifting immortal and all that bawdy business – let's just say that this wasn't the *only* thing he kept hidden in his desk. The other thing was a bottle of booze which he'd often nip when no one was standing directly behind him. How else was a writer supposed to make it through each day as an editor?

"Double scotch on the rocks, please" he informed the flight attendant after she asked him for his drink order. This he took from her and immediately tossed down his

Editorial

throat, but still the ideas continued to come. When the cart came wheeling back down the aisle for the second time, he ordered two scotches more. He couldn't help but notice how incredibly funny and absurd it was that they were going through the motions of an actual drink service for their one and only passenger, but nevertheless he was glad they hadn't cancelled it. Suddenly, an entire short story based on the incident flashed into his brain. He'd have to hurry...

The two drinks he tossed down the instant he had them in his hands, first the left and then the right. Before the flight attendant could wheel her cart back up to the front of the plane, where it would surely be lost to him for good, he had her by the hem of her dress.

"Wait, please..." he begged feebly, trying not to look at her face for the novella it contained.

"Yes?" she replied, as politely and professionally as she could while removing his hands from her person.

"I'd like another scotch."

"But sir..."

"Please, I need it."

"But you've just had four in a row!"

"Just one more, please..."

She shoved the drink into his hands and took off with the cart before he could accost her again, locking it in the cabinet up front and taking her seat beside the door to the cockpit. She was having a hard time disguising her disapproval of him by this point, but he didn't really care – it wasn't as if her approval was going to save them. With trembling hands Ed brought the glass to his lips, draining it with no apparent movement or effort of any kind. Unfortunately, he realized, as the mountains became visible through the floor, it was already too late.

36.

Perhaps one would've expected a sudden hole to erupt in the side of the plane, or maybe the entire fuselage to tear in half dramatically, but Ed was no Hollywood screenwriter. Not that he wouldn't have accepted the job had it been offered (goodbye editor's salary!), but Ed was the kind of writer who was obligated to write about things *imaginatively*, and the less he had to drink the more imaginative his writing became. Therefore, Ed could only write the plane away altogether, slowly and steadily fading into nothingness, leaving him, the flight attendant, the pilot and co-pilot flying along without it instead.

Just in case Hollywood was watching, however, he would instigate some action by having the entire flight crew plummet to their deaths from four miles up. This he accomplished by arranging for their eventual observation of the facts. So, five lines and fifteen minutes later:

THE PLANE!!!

As they all fell screaming, Ed caught a glimpse up (down?) the flight attendant's skirt, which caused his cock to rise a little. Still, he resisted his baser instinct to rewrite her back up to his altitude, possibly to use as a romantic interest later in the script. Hollywood may have been watching, but a writer had to retain *some* kind of integrity!

Partly due to his own unwillingness to commit suicide, but mostly because it made for a better story, Ed did not write the same fate for himself. And yet, not much else could happen now that the both the setting and all but one the characters had been cut from the scene. So, in keeping with the décor of such a high flying scenario, he wrote *himself* into an aircraft of sorts, but not as some lame transforming robot or anything to that effect. In fact, Ed the aircraft remained pretty much the same as Ed the human, still in the shape of a man sitting down even, cutting up and down through the clouds for alternating views of the sun and earth.

Just for fun though, he wrote in a toilet to replace his invisible seat and put his pants down around his ankles, so it made more sense. At this point he could tell for sure that he hadn't had nearly enough to drink, for the ideas were REALLY starting to flow!

Just then Ed's favorite contemporary American author flew by on a crapper of his own, only his had a small desk with a typewriter built into the front of it. But before Ed could ask for his autograph, the haggard old drunk took a swig of red wine and flipped him the bird, sneering wickedly as he passed him on the left, causing a draft that nearly sent him into a spin. Then, suddenly falling back and ascending to a piece of airspace just above Ed's head, the author let loose one of his legendary beer shits, glorious and stinking.

It seemed that Ed would get his autograph after all!

This same anal afterburner (completely coating the protective force field Ed wrote up at the last moment) sent the author jetting off almost at the speed of sound, disappearing in an instant into the wild blue yonder.

"Don't try!" was all he said before he left for good.

Fortunately, Ed did not need to write in window wipers, or some other self-cleaning mechanism, flying as fast as he was up so high as he was – the stratosphere took care of it for him. Within seconds his ship was completely clean, the force field sterilized by the fire in the ice, thus allowing him to continue his maiden flight unsullied. He could hold no grudge though; in fact he could only feel honored that a writer of such stature would deign to use him (of all writers) as a launch pad to wherever it was he was going. It was at this point that Ed realized with some regret the loss of all that frozen putrid shit which had been so neatly chipped away by the combined effects of temperature, friction, and velocity. Even a single gram of authentic famous dead author shit would have net him enough money to enter comfortable retirement tomorrow.

But Ed Duvall wasn't interested in retirement, as young as he was – he was interested in WORK. Work was what kept a man *sane*, this man anyway…

Work, and *drinking*.

It is perhaps no small secret that many writers are also alcoholics, drug addicts, or habitual wearers of blue jeans. Well, it may not surprise the reader to learn that a certain percentage of these writers use these things, these habits, as a source of inspiration in their work. This isn't to say that they couldn't write without them (if they were any good in the first place), it was just that certain things were capable of unlocking new insights and potentials in the writer. After all, is it even possible to imagine Kerouac's *On the Road* without massive doses of Benzedrine, or Shakespeare's *Sonnets* without the inspiration of a certain "Fair Youth"?

Anyway, whatever else separated Ed Duvall from the truly great writers, there was another crucial aspect in which he was fundamentally opposite. Whereas there was

Editorial

certainly no shortage of the type of writer mentioned above, Ed was the rare writer (possibly the only writer) who *never* used booze or anything else as a crutch for his imagination. Quite to the contrary – he used it as a sledgehammer.

And right about now he was starting to realize that he'd hardly had enough to constitute a rubber mallet.

He realized this because now his aircraft was equipped with a massive energy cannon in the shape of a monstrous, bulging cock, the head represented by an enormous oblong heat sink at its tip, with veins encircling the long, high-caliber barrel in the form of various tubes and wire conduits. With each pulse of pure blue creative potential it shot forth, spermatozoa-like rounds were continuously reloaded from the dual spherical ammunition batteries which also served as its base.

Impressive for a cannon of its size and strength, it was capable of firing off 0.8 loads per second.

But all of this was purely schematic, superficial information compared to what the thing could actually *do*. I suspect that the fact of it taking the form of exaggerated male genitalia is largely incidental. It is not as if a female writer, writing a story about a male writer writing a story, necessarily would've chosen something different. Either way God was creation and, for the male character anyway, the cock was the closest accessible representation of that creation. And every writer considers himself or herself to be God, in a sense, reshaping the world in their own image (or that of their genitalia) in however many days and nights of work and rest were necessary.

Whatever the case, it may well be that a cunt cannon would've been better suited to the task. Of course, according to this plan the cock cannon – immense and powerful as it seemed by itself – would need to be relegated to a subordinate position, maybe as a clip supplying bullets which could only be processed and put to good use through the barrel of the birth canal.

No wonder all of Ed's best ideas came out half-baked…

Regardless of the limitations inherent in his inferior equipment, Ed was really sowing the seed up there! A blast of blue – cumulous clouds cum crystalline concepts – a castle here, a whale there – and yet always falling (as ice usually does) back down to earth, either to crash into the ocean, melt back into water before even penetrating the inner atmosphere, or strike land and become, if only for the instant it took to shatter, part of the *real* world for once.

A stoned teenager, lying across the hood of a car, turns to the other stoned teenager who owns the car and says:
"Hey… Do you see that giant up there?"
"No…"
"Serious dude! Look, it's a giant man peeking through a tiny doorway!"
"Oh yeah…"

Editorial

Blue bullets of *ENERGY MIND MAGIC* going off left and right, and yet for every thought born of Father Sky, just another miscarried stillborn aborted bastard plummeting down, down, down to the Earth Mother he never had… This must've been a metaphor for his own life and work, Ed thought to himself, right before he woke up/passed out.

37.

When the plane landed in Miami, Ed got off with the rest of the passengers, "deboarding" in an orderly fashion, then found the baggage claim, claimed his bags, and hailed a taxi – just like any normal person on their way into town.

"Ferré and 15th, please."

The flat was up a few flights of stairs from street level. Ed knocked on the door at the end of the dingy hallway: Apartment #401.

The inside of the apartment was just as dimly lit and sparsely decorated as the hall outside. The only piece of furniture in the whole place, as far as Ed could see, was a single miniature recliner with a busted foot rest that hung down to one side, situated in the center of a green, threadbare rug in the middle of the living room floor. A person was seated within it. Ed surmised, correctly, that this person was to be his client.

Though the recliner was clearly designed to accommodate a child, Ed's client was clearly much older. Or at least they seemed to be. At any rate the real issue at hand was that the client was obviously too large (not too old) for the chair, though Ed had to admit it was a little hard to tell... He took a couple of quick hits from the stainless steel flask in his coat pocket.

"Please, have a seat," the client instructed.

With no particular reason to disobey, Ed did as he was told and sat down on the rug before the recliner. They sat there together like that for some time, just looking at each other. Ed took another hit of his bourbon. Still he could not explain exactly what his client looked like.

"What is it that you want me to do, exactly?" Ed asked, "For the job, that is."

He went to unscrew the cap of his flask once again, forgetting that it was already open. He took the last half hit and placed it back into his pocket, trying hard to focus on his client's amorphous facial features.

"You are Mr.... ahh, Mrs...."

It was no use at all.

"You are the one who sent for me, correct?"

"Correct."

Editorial

Finally!

"So why is it that you've sent for me? What exactly would you have me do?"

"Do?"

"Yes. Do. For the *job*."

"The job…"

"Yes, the job! The job you sent for me to do."

"What exactly is your occupation, Mr. Duvall?"

"I'm an edi… well, I'm a writer. I write things, sometimes for other people. Is that why you've brought me here? Because you'd like for me to write something for you?"

"Yes."

"Well, what would you like me to write?"

Nothing.

"Well?"

"Well what?"

"What am I to write?"

"Oh, sorry, I was thinking of something else…"

"Your money, pal."

Things went on like this for some time. Ed's ass was beginning to go numb from sitting on the hard floor for so long. Finally, when he'd had just about enough and was ready to leave (to where he did not know), the client finally let it slip:

"I'd like for you to write my life story."

Ed let go of the door handle, turned around slowly, and retook his seat on the rug in front of the recliner. His ass immediately began to go numb once again.

"You mean like a biography?"

Nothing.

38.

Ed found a room above a bar just a few blocks down the street and went to work that very night. His client, though apparently living quite an austere lifestyle in that little empty apartment of theirs, was actually quite fabulously well-to-do. Not only had they paid his room in advance for several months, they had provided him with an electric typewriter and a generous weekly stipend for spending money as well. Most of this he wisely spent downstairs, lest his client's "life story" took a turn like the airplane episode from before.

Ed had thought it best to sit down with his client every week or so, partly so that he could interview them and take notes, but mainly so that he could collect his money in a timely manner. Each time they sat down to talk, Ed would ask his client different questions concerning various periods of the life they'd led up until that point. Ed would then use the information gleaned from these interviews as raw material for the life story he was writing. Yet it seemed that the more notes he took, the further away he got from the true essence of the story, which was proving to be just as fleeting and ephemeral as his client's mercurial features.

Despite writing down and embellishing upon every detail of his client's life, Ed was making remarkably little headway on the book he was trying to write for them. It had already been a month and he'd only managed to write a few disparate fragments – hardly even a full chapter to show for all his efforts.

Editorial

A few days later Ed went for his weekly stipend collection/interview with his client. They were interested to hear what kind of progress he'd been making.

"Progress..." Ed began, staring blankly into the glass of good scotch in his hand, "Progress is going well."
"Can I see it?"
"See what?"
"Your progress so far."
"Well..."
"Well what?"
"It's just that I don't like to let the cat out of the bag prematurely, you know?"
"No, I don't know."
"Well, you've heard the old expression 'loose lips sink ships,' haven't you?"
"Yes, I have."
"Well, let's just say that this life story of yours is gonna be one big *bastard* of a ship, and I'd hate to ruin it by talking about it too much before it's ready to come out of the oven."

"Unacceptable."

Following this incident, Ed's weekly stipend was cut in half, leaving him with just enough money for food, other basic necessities, and a few daily drinks. This was decided by his client, not out of any real dissatisfaction or desire to punish, but simply out of pure necessity. For his client understood, as Ed suspected, that there was really only one way they were going to get the kind of life story they wanted out of him.

"Well," Ed grumbled, setting down his empty bottle and loading a fresh sheet of paper into the typer, "you asked for it, you son of a bitch…"

39.

So Ed sobered up – for the most part, anyway. Since he was never as physically addicted as he was mentally, this didn't even prove to be that big of a challenge, given the demands of his peculiar client. In fact, things had gotten to the point where Ed specifically saved his nips for the points where the narrative *categorically* went off track. Most of the time now, he just needed a little sauce here and there for the sake of coherence and continuity.

Editorial

These being relative terms, of course.

He had managed to write half a dozen well-revised chapters within a week of resuscitating his (now carefully controlled) creative potential, which had been undergoing a long, sustained drowning in a pool of other spirits until quite recently. He was getting better at harnessing his visions, he found, and relied on the bottle less and less for the dissipation of his more frightening conceptions.

Were he to lapse into a flight of fancy as terrifying and absurd as the airplane incident again, he was sure now that he could handle it. However, just in case, he always made sure to keep a bottle nearby, lest he inadvertently write something completely inappropriate about his client's imaginary life.

Ed had never written in the biographical genre before, but he was beginning very much to enjoy it – especially since he was given license to make most of it up as he went. But then, this work wasn't all that different from that of the historian, really, whose writing often showed less esteem for the truth than that of the average novelist.

The fact was that his client hadn't given him very much to work with. In spite of his in-depth questioning and meticulous note taking, Ed had retained very little raw material from the time he had spent researching his client's life. One would assume that the best way to write a good biography would be to talk extensively with the person to be biographed and then write it all down in a fitting style. This was exactly what Ed had thought. Yet his client had proven to be such a tough nut to crack, such a non-entity, such a blank slate *tabla rasa* vanilla bean (if the expression will be pardoned) that there would not have been enough character in an entire industrial-sized bucket of vanilla extract – distilled from this client – to make up so much as an obituary, let alone an entire life story.

Perhaps this was the true crux of the issue. But then, perhaps Ed was just a lousy interviewer/note taker, and an even lousier writer at that...

It would not be unreasonable to say that both statements were simultaneously true!

Whatever Ed lacked in talent, however, he more than made up for with his natural penchant for creativity. And whatever his client lacked in interesting experience, they more than made up for in raw potential. And so the ultimate alliance was forged. The ultimate biography – completely unrestrained by the biographed life *or* the biographer's capacity to embellish upon it.

Not that he needed it for the purposes of this current project, but Ed just so happened to be sitting on some pretty good unpublished material already. So, he figured, why not rework it a little?

When he wasn't writing about his client's experience as an elderly Chilean child molester or a blastocyst at a bisexual baby shower, Ed was able to concoct an entire history in which everything that could conceivably happen to a person *happened*. In order to make this story believable, however, he had to reconcile his client's seemingly unlimited propensity for experience with their (presumed) mortality.

So he made his client immortal.

Easy.

Editorial

Still, in order to make this decidedly unlikely trait believable, he would have to find some way of explaining it. People were generally willing to believe anything so long as it was explained to them in an authoritative tone. If it were explained to them in an authoritative tone by a man in a silly robe or hat, they would believe even more still. And if it were explained to them in a *flattering* light, there was literally no end to what people would accept as truth, especially with regard to themselves. But then, Ed's account of his client's endless, all-encompassing life wasn't always what one would call flattering (how could it be?), so if it were his client he was trying to convince, he would have to adopt an especially authoritative tone for this one...

Of course, Ed blew that chance almost immediately.

In the process of explaining how his client first gained immortality, which would've been precisely the same moment his parents and sister officially fulfilled their mortality, Ed made the mistake of offering a rather wide range for the age his client had achieved by that point in time. Any respectable reader, of course, one who wasn't already a total fool (or willing to be made one of), would expect much more out of their narrator as far as credibility was concerned. Either they knew, or they didn't, correct? And if they didn't even know the age of the main character, at such a pivotal moment as the achievement of immortality (like dying and going to Heaven [*sound of the choir singing*]), then how could they be relied upon to recall and convey accurately the other significant details (and less significant details) of the protagonist's story? Surely this narrator was a fraud!

But supposing there was a more sophisticated reader out there, one not quite so reactionary or prone to jumping to conclusions…

Supposing.

40.

The first thing he felt, after the impact of the seatbelt against his waist and chest, nearly lacerating his skin, was the intense heat of the gasoline-fueled flames, already consuming his parents in what used to be the front seat of their family sedan. Now, it was only the second bottommost compartment of broken glass and burning steel in the seven car pile up on Interstate 77. He was in the bottommost.

The first thing he saw, after the aforementioned – the globules of melted fat dripping from his mother's arm; the finer details of his father's shattered spinal column – was his sister, sitting in the seat beside him. She wore her hair in pigtails and held a popsicle in one had, eating it calmly. Attempting to ask her *are you alright*, perhaps he wasn't quite so surprised as he should've been to find that he could no longer hear his own voice…

With a knowing smile upon her face, his sister took a good long lick of the orange ice cream push-pop in her hand. It was getting *hot* in the backseat now, hot enough by any standard. At this point she turned and offered him a lick – a boon he felt compelled to accept without hesitation.

Editorial

Later, when he was found wandering on the side of the road, without so much as a scratch on his body, no one could even believe at first that he had been involved in the accident. He remained in police custody until two days later, when it came his parent's turn to have their teeth identified by the coroner. Then, shortly after the proper contacts were established and the necessary arrangements were made, he was claimed by his aunt and uncle.

Only he didn't recognize them as such.

It wasn't until much later in his stay with them that he realized their true identities – demonic doppelganger caretakers (having replaced his REAL aunt and uncle) working in the employ of the DEVIL, whom (of course!) had presented himself in the form of his pig-tailed, popsicle-licking little sister in the backseat of *Hell* just a few years prior. How else could these apparent strangers have known his name, or that his parents had just been killed, or where to find him so soon after the fact?

Having forfeited his eternal soul in exchange for the right to live following his father's mishap behind the wheel that fateful day, he knew that there was little he could do to renege now – the deal had been sealed with a lick of an orange-flavored popsicle.

His father, incidentally, was not a very good father at all, but rather like most fathers – that is to say, better at being a standard person than any type of *special* person (like a father). His chief interest was in himself, like most people. And really, compared to what his son had to offer, who could blame him?

Long before the day he was born had the days passed when a parent could expect a modicum of work (or even just basic respect) out of their children. Instead, their children constituted an enormous DRAG on both their patience and their pocketbooks, a condition exasperated even more by a society that on one hand defined the quality of a child's life in dollars, and on the other measured a parent's parentworthiness by the amount of unlimited, unconditional (ha!) love they were able to provide in the face of pure hatred and resentment.

He often felt sorry for his dad, really, when he considered how many of his personal goals and dreams he

Editorial

must've abandoned to work full-time in a textile factory, listen to non-stop crying, change dirty diapers, hear pitiful requests for useless items in the supermarket, and practically give up fucking mom altogether just on account of *him*, for the short few years they knew each other before his death.

As far as his mother was concerned, she was not much different. Like most other females of her generation (or any generation), she knew better, but nevertheless allowed herself to be sucked into the same prescribed nonsense as the rest of her foremothers, and all for the lack of a better idea (or the means of fulfilling it). In her defense, however, it must be admitted that it was not *her* idea to have unprotected sex with a man she had only recently met, let alone get married and have children with him. Like most women, she was the victim of both man's tyranny and her own complacency within it. Still, this did not make her any different from the hordes of lesser men who bent over to be fucked daily by their own masters, expected to produce babies of a more profitable nature as the wheels of the economic machine turned and turned.

At least somebody finally figured out how to make their kids pay for themselves (and then some)!

In fact, there were many of these lesser men in American factories (which moved to Southeast Asia long before the collapse) who were capable of giving birth to as many as 500 automobiles, 50,000 pairs of socks, and 5,000,000 toothpicks *each and every day* of their economically reproductive lives! Many of them lost their ability to reproduce biologically, however, as a consequence of spending too much time in said factories. When their masters found out about this, it wasn't so much the class action lawsuits or humanitarian concerns that compelled them to clean things up to the point where infertility rates dropped to an acceptable level – it was the fact that if their slaves were no longer able to reproduce *biologically*, then eventually there would be no one left to reproduce for them *economically* either.

Who could they fuck, day in and day out, to populate the earth with more cornflakes, mp3 players, and deodorant soaps (which would be consumed by the next generation of slaves and their offspring, and their offspring) if the current generation of slaves all went biologically infertile?

The lifecycle as human earthlings had known it since the Industrial Revolution would grind to a groaning halt, and, having nothing left to produce or consume, all of them (master and slave alike) would shortly kill themselves out of sheer boredom. Of course, the Great Collapse would take care of this for them, long before the world economy ceased creating the necessary replicants.

But now we're officially getting ahead of ourselves!

41.

There were a number of years (let's be honest; we don't know how many) that he lived in the extra room on the second floor of his aunt and uncle's house, there on that miraculously tall hill so far inland from the world's vast oceans. How tall would this hill have to have been, anyway, in order to peek its head above the coming cataclysmic flood, to have its sole structure survive along with the most high-up-there houses of the Himalayas?

Editorial

Well, if those are the sorts of questions that the reader is going to ask, then perhaps they should purchase a copy of the Bible, or a scientific book on climate and geography, and let me get on with my story.

The point (one point) is that there were a number of years after he was orphaned which he spent collecting pornographic magazines. Many of these were likely stolen from his uncle's own collection, the rest of which were likely obtained (stealthily under his shirt and inconspicuously out the door) from the gas station down the road, or else bartered for chewing gum and baseball cards from his classmates at school.

Did I mention he attended school?

One may have received the impression that our protagonist never left the house at all until the day he was finally cast out, based on his seeming naiveté with regard to just about every object and occurrence around him, but no, he did in fact attend school quite often – when he wasn't busy masturbating. Occasionally he would masturbate at school as well, but this was sometimes difficult and always less than ideal, as the number and variety of pornographic magazines he was able to keep stashed in the bottom of his locker was far inferior to what he had at home, hidden securely in the large trunk which he kept beneath his bed.

So, to prevent the reader from having to wonder any further, I hereby present the following episode from his school days – this relates the time he was caught masturbating beneath the bleachers during gym class, *and* the way in which he craftily convinced his teacher not to write him up for suspension:

42.

XX XXX X XXXX XXX XXXX XX XX XXXX XXX XXXXX, XX XXXX XX XXX XXX XXXXXX XXX XXX XXXXX XXXXXX XXXXXXXXXX XX XXX XXXXX XXXX XX XXXXXX XXX.

XX XXXXXX XXXX XX XXXXX X XXXX XX XXX XXXXXXX XXXXXXXX XX XX XXX XXXXXXX XXXX XX XXXXXX X XXX XXXX XXX XXXX XXX XX XXXXXX.

XXXX XXX X XXXXXX XXXX XX XXX XXXX XXXX XX XX XXXX XX XXXX XXX XXXXXXXX XXX XXXXXXX XXXXXX XX XXXXXX XXXX XXXXX XXXXX XXXXXX XXX XXX XXX XXXX XX XXX XXXX XX XX XXXX'X XX XXXXXXXX XXXX XX XXXX XX, XXXX XX XXX XXXX XXXXX XXX XXXXXX, XXXX XX XXX XXXX XXXXX XXX XXXXXXX, XX XXXX XX XXXXX XXX XXXXXXXX XXX XXXXX XXXXXXXX X XXXXXX XXXXX XX XXX XXXX XXXXXXX XXXX XX XXX XXXX'X XXXX XXXX.

XXXX XXX XX XXX XXXX XX XXXXX XX XXXX XX XXX XXX XX XXXX, XXXX.

XX XXXX'X XXXX XXXX XXX XXX XX XXX XXX XXXXXXX XXXX XXXXXX XXX XXXXXXX XXXX XXX XXXXXX XXXX XX XXX XXXX. XXX XXXX XXXX XXXX XXX XXXX XXXX XX, XXXXX XXX, XXX XXXX. XX XXXX XXXXX XX XXXXXX XXXX XXX XX XXXX XXXXX XX XXXX, XX XXXXX, XXXXXX XXXX XXX XXXX XXX XXXX XXXX XXX XXXXXXX'X XXXXXX XXXX XXX XXXX.

Editorial

XXX XXX XXXXX XXX XXXX XXXX XXXXXXXX XX XXX. XXXX XXXXXXXX XXXX XXX XXX XXXXXX XXX XXXXXXX XXXXX XX XXXX XXXX X XXX XXXXXXXX XXXXXX. XXXXX XXX XXX XXXX, XX XXXXXXX XXX XXX XXXXXXX XXXX XX XXX XXXXXXXX XXX XXXXX XXX XX XXXXX XXX XXXX, XXXXX XXX XXX XXXXXXX XX XXXXXX XXX XX XXXXX.

"XXXX XXXX XX XXX XXXXX XX XXXXX'X XX XXXXX XXXX?" XX XXXXX. XX XXXXX XXXX XXX XXXXXX XXX XXXXXXX XXXXXXXX XXX XXXXX XX XXXXXX XXXX XXXX XXXXXXXX XXXX XXXX XXXXXXXX XX XXXX XXXX XXXXXXXX XXX XXXXXXXX XXX XXXX XXX XXXXXXXX, XX XXXX XX XXX XXXXXXXX XXXX XXX XXXX. XXXXXXX XXXX.

XXXX XX XXXX XX XXXX XXXX XX XXXX XXX XXXXXXXX'X XXXXXX XXXX XXX, XXX XXXX XXX XX XXX XXXXXXXXXX, XXX XX XXX XXXXXX XXXXXXXXXX XX XXX XX-XXXXXX XXXXXXXX XXX XXXXXXXXXXXX XXXXXXX.

And that was the end of that.

43.

It has since come to my attention that something strange happened in the conveyance of the episode above. Some readers have complained to me that the preceding chapter is entirely blank, which is impossible because I remember writing it, and it was not written in invisible ink (some readers were able to verify as much when their special glasses, paper treatments, and various other methods failed to produce anything). A few others wrote in or called to say that the pages in their copies had been removed entirely, ripped out by some anonymous vandal, or else left out of the binding process altogether. This to me seems a bit more plausible, but still quite absurd.

Still others have written emails to the publisher to ask why there is one chapter written in German or Vietnamese or Spanish or some other "an" or "ese" or "ish" in the otherwise English language book they bought. I handle all of these messages personally, often responding via telegram or passenger pigeon (just to piss them off) with the simple response:

"You must've bought the ___ an/ese/ish version by mistake. So sorry!"
To which they usually reply, once again via email:
"No, I didn't."
To which I reply via Pony Express post card:
"Yes, you did!"

A week or two usually go by, after which I inevitably receive a small parcel in the mail (15-52 arriving almost every day) containing their copy of the book along with a brief letter demanding their money back. These I put back into their packaging – carefully resealed so as to avoid paying return postage – and stamp in red ink "RETURN TO SENDER" after enclosing a form letter, of which I have preprinted thousands:

> *We are sorry to inform you that your 30 day money back guarantee has expired.*

Jackpot!

RETURN TO SENDER

44.

After aunt and uncle gave his client the boot, Ed wrote – trying hard to resist the emergency bottle locked in the desk drawer – what they did next was a matter of contention.

According to his client, they "wandered around for a while." According to Ed, they spent two months traversing the desert between their former home and a truck stop after being transformed into a snake, eating only five times along the way due to their inexperience hunting rodents. What is generally agreed upon (reported in the local paper, dated XXX XXth, 19XX) is that Ed's client entered the Oasis truck stop, halfway between XXXXXXXXXX, XX, and Reno, NV, wearing nothing but a ragged blue tarp. According to several eyewitness accounts, they were last seen leaving in a station wagon driven by a salesman wearing a brown and yellow checkered jacket.

Whose side to believe?

As outlandish as Ed's version of the story surrounding his client's departure proved to be, it must be stated in his defense that he wasn't given much to go on in the first place. If he was forced to embellish a small bit...

It should also be noted that in their collaborations, during which Ed would periodically submit chapters to his client for review, he was never once corrected or rebuked for making false or misleading claims about their life. As in any group enterprise, there were a host of minor changes to be made, but these had more to do with the smaller details involved, such as the texture of a surface, or the color of some piece of clothing, than any questions of basic narrative veracity. As his client saw it, Ed was doing a wonderful job of telling their life story. The interviews they submitted to provided all the raw material Ed needed to do his job as biographer (provided he laid off the sauce), and who better to provide these materials than the client? As long as Ed didn't get *too* creative in his editing, his client kept perfect faith in what he was doing. And why shouldn't they have? Ed had already edited countless other stories written by other people, and he had written a book of his own as well...

Editorial

Ed *had* written a book of his own, he seemed to recall, back when he was still drinking continuously, relying on the bottle to keep his most unbearable (and unpublishable) thoughts from the printed page. Now that he was more accustomed to focusing his creative process without having to drown 90% of his output in a deluge of less inspiring spirits, he wondered what he might've done with this book had he been able to think more clearly during its composition...

The tolerance for alcohol he'd developed in that time left him less and less able to self censor even as his intake of booze grew steadily more more more – no human being could be expected to continue at that rate and not die as a result. It was a good thing he had taken the job in Miami, he thought, because if he hadn't, he never would've learned how to edit without the drink, the solvent which separated the gold from the raw ore of his nonstop dizzying inspirations.

Now, for instance, he could think back on some of the more memorable scenes he had written, memorable mostly for their wild and incoherent beauty, and derive from them something more accessible, more pedestrian – more *printable*. Now that he had a client, one whom had commissioned him to write a biography of an essentially unbiographical (as yet unlived) life, it occurred to him that perhaps he already had written his client's immense and all-encompassing story; maybe he had somehow channeled everything out of this mysterious stranger's mind, and now that they had finally met face to face, they would finally be able to sort out fact from fiction and produce something which was, if nothing else, readable.

Maybe he was losing it again; maybe he would have to ask his client for a larger expense account.

To test this theory – the latter half of it anyway – Ed sat down at his desk, wet his tongue with the last few drops of gin left in his contingency bottle, and began working on the chapter he'd begun earlier that day. This was the chapter detailing his client's experience as a traveling salesman in the western United States, particularly the events of one day spent in Reno, Nevada.

45.

"Man my dick sure was sore when I woke up this mornin' whoo boy I tell ya—after that fag I picked up on the way down here n' all my whackin' off to the TV n' humpin' my gosh darned mattress all night on top of it (don't know what's gotten into me lately!)—I'm about as raw as a pound of raw hamburger meat only that's been left to cook in the sun a bit.

But shit that don't mean these deliveries orders demonstrations n' courtesy calls gonna deliver order demonstrate n' call all by themselves now do it—so I goes back over my list one last time puts a little ointment on my pecker checks out at the front desk n' hits the road hopin' I gets done early enough so's I can make my show—but boy if Reno hasn't changed!

Between all the wetback construction crews buildin' this up n' tearin' that down it's like tryin' to navigate a whole new city—seems like every turn I take is takin' me left n' ever left n' hell by the time I've done my first delivery the whole danged city's done changed once again—this time with a new road curvin' off to the

Editorial

left ever left n' my car in a vacant lot off to the side where the old road used to been goddamnit—I get in n' follow the curve to my next few stops before I decide it's time for lunch so I goes lookin' for my favorite old lunch stand which I find with great surprise right where I expect on 118 East n' I order my pork sandwich n' sit down in the adjoinin' park to eat n' while I'm washin' the whole mess down with a diet cola I realize that this town really ain't all that different than I remember it bein' last time I came through n' really must be *me* that's havin' the problem here—must be workin' too damn hard I reckon what with all them long days n' nights on the road but if so that's a sorry thing as you'd expect I'd have more to show for it by now whoo boy!

So I gets up but before I goes I decides I'd like a cookie for the road n' they got the *best* damned molasses cookies at this here particular lunch stand almost as good as grandma's in fact though I'd never say so to her face (God rest her soul) n' as I tip the kid behind the counter he smiles n' I'll be damned if he ain't got fangs in his teeth—must be one of them crazy new fashions kids always be coming out with can't understand nor do I even have the time n' energy to keep up with it so I just says if the kids wanna have fangs or piercin's or buttcracks hangin' all out their pants they can knock themselves out havin' all the fun they want lookin' like a bunch of dumb asses n' there ain't no thing I can do about it any damn way so why worry.

I got my change from the fanged freak n' hit the road once more this time knockin' out several more orders demos n' deliveries without event only now this ever leftward-leading road has really got me thinkin' this whole damned *city's* been taken off it's grid n' rearranged in a circle—what in the holy hell—n' furthermore the asphalt has all been replaced by brown n' yellow cobblestones it seems as my tires go BUMP BUMP BUMP BUMP over them only the pattern they've been laid in more closely resembles the scales of a snake n' I can only think to myself by golly this town's done lost it's damned *mind* (or perhaps I've lost mine) as I dutifully continue on to my last stop with nothin' more than a shake of my head n' a shrug of my shoulders to express my utter disgust n' confusion.

With no difficulty at all I manage to find my last stop though this has nothin' to do with my sense of direction n' everythin' to do with my blind faith at this point that if I just keep followin' that curve to the left I'd get there which sure enough I did—can't hardly bear to look at what they done to the beautiful flat black road all done up now to look like some damned dinosaur as I steps out the car so I closes my eyes n' damn near trips over the goddamned curb which thankfully still looks just like it's supposed to I notice as I open my eyes n' this gives me no end of relief as you might imagine.

In the lobby of the buildin' I am greeted by a receptionist who thank God looks like a *proper* young lady with proper mammal teeth not a fang among them not even particularly sharp canines for that matter so for a moment I feel as if I am sane *but not for long* because no sooner than I make it past security do I notice—whoo boy look out shoulda seen *this* one comin'—but I'll be damned if the folks in here men n' women alike custodial to business dress all got these hideous RATTLES hangin' right out the front flaps of their pants or the hem of their skirts n' even special butt flaps for some man n' woman alike don't matter n' as soon as I notice this they all seem to instantly notice me as if by pheromonal telepathy n' no sooner than this recognition becomes mutual does the awful mass RATTLIN' begin...

RATTLE RATTLE RATTLE RATTLE RATTLE RATTLE RATTLE RATTLE RATTLE RATTLE RATTLE

At first it's kind of subtle like I'm not sure it's happenin' right away like so much of this thoroughly BIZARRE day but no such luck I'm afraid because just as soon as one starts rattlin' another does too n' after two there's four n' after four there's sixteen n' you do the math it's exponential—next thing I know I gots a whole gang of riled up office snake den workers shakin' their awful THINGS at me n' to make matters worse they all got this LOOK in their yellow vertical insane eyeballs like as if they're fixin' to EAT me alive—no thank you— so right about now I'm headin' out the way I came but by this point the rattlin' has reached quite a pitch like a crescendo only instead of subsidin' it just continues to build n' build until I'm sure I can't stand no more of these SATANIC hallucination monkeyshines as if I am the unwittin' victim of some very juvenile n' very tasteless (but at the same time very sophisticated n' elaborate) practical joke but just as soon as I'm sure enough is enough I feel somethin' stabbin' me in the buttocks n' sure enough it's some clerk with his rattle goin' after my fundament as if to enter it but I'll be damned if—but no faster than I can turn around to slug the crazed dumb FAGGOT do I feel *another* rattle pokin' at my side only to find out it's a WOMAN comin' after me (my anal canal) n' I swear I never felt so damned sickened in all my days by such a degenerate in all my time not even anywhere up n' down this coast I been workin' all these years amongst nothin' but SINNERS.

Somehow I gets out of there but before I reach the end of that gantlet I feels as though I been stabbed, poked, or otherwise prodded n' molested in every imaginable every which way—seven ways to Sunday even—by thoroughly ABOMINABLE abominations with their hard, leathery rattles protrudin' from their crotchal zones n' fingertips n' sometimes nose n' tonguetips…

I step carefully off the curb n' over the scales of the street which are positively the scales of a snake now undulatin' in a great serpentine motion n' into my car which is still there somehow rockin' back n' forth upon that stretch of scales far as the eye can see in this town gone positively MAD which starts miraculously n' without warnin' transformin' into a SNAKE right before my very eyes but as I adjust the rearview mirror before pullin' out into traffic—hopin' to get the hell out of there n' quick—I can tell from the fangs n' the scales n' the eyes which meet mine that it is already too damned late ah well."

46.

Ed had dinner with his client that evening, after which he showed them the chapter he'd been working on. He'd hoped that he could use this latest disaster as proof that his ability to control his wilder flights of fancy was, if not on the wane, at least temporarily plateaued, and that upping his intake of alcohol, LSD, or *something* may be the only way to stabilize him and dampen his creativity to the point where he could avoid producing such insane ramblings in the future.

Ed's client put the binder down next to the salad bowl and looked at it sitting there.

"So," Ed began, "what do you think?"
"Think?"
"Yes, think."
"Of this?" the client asked, indicating the binder.
"Yes. What do you think of it."
"I think it's perfect."
"Really?"
"Yes, really."
"I must admit that isn't the reaction I expected."
"And what reaction did you expect?"
"Well, certainly not that."
"Perfect?" the client asked.
"Yes," Ed answered.
"So you agree then?"
"Huh?"
"I'm glad you see what a great work of art you've produced."
"But that's not…" Ed began to protest.

"It's perfect!"
"…what I meant."
"Son I don't think it needs any more."
"What do you mean?"
"I mean I think you've captured it."
"Captured it?"
"Yes, captured it."
"But what could you possibly mean by *it* here?"
"I mean what *happened*."
"But you've never even been to Reno!"
"Beside the point."

Things weren't going the way Ed had hoped, to say the least.

"But how can you call this an accurate representation of what *happened*?"
"I don't follow."
"Nothing like this has ever happened to anyone!"
"It hasn't?"
"It couldn't."
"But how can you say that when the proof is right here in front of you?"
"Proof? This is a work of *fiction*."
"Isn't everything though?"
"I am LOSING it…" Ed groaned.
"But look at what we've *gained*!"
"…I need DRINK."
"You need to *listen*."
"…"
"Listen."
"Alright, I'm listening."
"Alright then, hear me out."
"Out with it then!"

Editorial

"There are essentially two types of people in this world – those who believe in choice and those who believe in fate."

"Okay."

"Would you at least agree that these two types of people hold beliefs which are basically contradictory?"

"For most intents and purposes, yes, probably."

"And can you tell me why that is?"

"I thought I was the one hearing *you* out!"

"Well, essentially, those who believe in fate presuppose a world where everything is laid out ahead of time in a logical order, and those who believe in choice assume that – no matter what natural laws happen to be at the moment – all things are changeable."

"That seems self explanatory enough."

"But there is a *third* type of person that I neglected to mention…"

"Okay."

"…and that is the type of person who believes in *possibility*."

"Alright."

"And why do you suppose this person believes what they believe?"

"You got me…"

"Well, on a long enough timeline, concepts like choice and fate become irrelevant."

"How do you figure?"

"Well, on a long enough timeline, all things become *possible*."

"I'm not quite sure I believe that."

"What's not to believe?"

"Just some things could never happen."

"What if they're fated?"

"They're not necessarily."
"Then what if they're chosen?"
"They needn't be."
"But still you'll have to admit that they all become possibilities on a long enough timeline."
"Well…"

47.

Ed was having a hard time debating this, if for no other reason than because it was a truism, and hence not really up for debate. Of course anything was possible – as unlikely as it seemed, the very laws of gravity could be nullified at any moment, and Ed could fall right up into the sky (or at least into his client's ceiling). However, he was having a hard time seeing how this little bit of axiomatic knowledge had any bearing on the biography at hand. Either his client had once been a traveling salesman who spent a rather eventful day in Reno, Nevada, or they had not – simple as that. Other questions of plausibility aside, his client couldn't possibly have been or done one thing, and something else simultaneously, could they have?

On a long enough timeline…

…not only did all things become *possible*, they became *inevitable*.

It is a common habit of thought that time is usually measured in length or width, but rarely depth. "Historian" (or in this case, "biographer") is the name given to the individual charged with plumbing the depths of time, taking each notable occurrence and describing it with the appropriate level of detail, context, and (perhaps most importantly) speculation. But whatever layers of cause and effect or strata of competing narratives are brought to light, the true fullness of history is invariably reduced to a flat, empty point on a timeline (or a chapter in a book) where it remains – dead, static – until the next brave soul dares to descend into its turbulent depths. As with all other things, consensus is tenuous and transitory at best.

So, given that so much is happening at every moment, and given that the interpretations of each moment are as numerous and varied as the uncountable beings (sentient and "nonsentient") experiencing them, and given that history repeats itself over and over again in seemingly infinite circular variations while at the same spontaneously generating and shifting from one dominant species, paradigm, and universe to the next, and given that on a long enough timeline not only did all things become possible, but in fact became inevitable, it wasn't *too* far of a stretch to say that one thing could be many different things (and maybe even *every*thing) all at once!

An old joke from British colonial India:

Q: What is the difference between a Hindoo and a Christian?

A: The former believes that everything is God, while the latter believes that God is everything.

48.

Victrola plays a snake scale ship song with blue balls rolling on red road sky thousand hundred years from book on birch bark disintegrated into blow sales job man on the coast going down to Himalaya high—says town pimp: "purple blimp"—now over relatively *un*troubled waters of the nation in a yellow and brown checkered screech sound of my first memory which was egg in butt (but butt ain't all) there is something printing bound in booze bottles of the scaliest days but cold fire makes more cash when you've been to Hell going round and round for the editorial privilege instilled in my ophidian teeth rattling out numbers in sequence—means nothing in the symbolic bumwot blast radius pleasingly unknown to the author oh *there.*

Cantonese passage read through sand he says "it's on me" but it's under Miami in actuality actually with the cunt cock dangling out more useless philosophy and numbers again with the years and dates with whores brass medals and regal busts of your favorite ass hole in the ground—wouldn't know it from flied lice—and your cat-fucking mother with reptammary glands suckling frogs and pigs alike in a bucket of nuclear war winter time in Reno Nevada has never been so hot girls in school on paper beneath mattresses in trunks with pigtails and popsicle transformations of flesh (money back guarantee no longer valid) from an energy cannon in the shape of a male member or pen scribbling personal post-apocalyptic histories—thoroughly impersonal mysteries—because everyone is dead in the past as well as the future XXX

Editorial

XXXX XX XXXXX XXXX'X XXX, XXXXXXX XXXXX XX XXX'X.

XXXX XX XXXX on the 14th floor going down while up on the lights in the faces off the polka mirror dots greenish grey mixture and furthermore a WOMAN has been elected but the men here have erected penis pen and power of atom in grain silos sowing seas and skies with seeds of red.

Bluish brown rusted parts no bueno with dots now like scales on dirt and skirt hiked up to his nipples disappearing nuts and eggs trailing primordial proteins from the rojas rattle red sands ringing the rectum of your mouth now live, now dead through rings of fire on the horizon with a round of applause heard round the whole round world now flat or almost (at sea level anyway)— mountains now mole hills upon a slick black mirror of stillness the whole planet now a great black marble lost down the black hole of space nothing so tumultuous about it now just another swampy cinder amongst trillions and *almost* as lifeless—could it be that mighty Ouroboros was winding the whole mess up for another go?

Fuck...

Well, that's certainly fitting, as all things begin and end with either this action or utterance. But whether it was the act or the word of copulation which preceded the beginning or end matters little here, because in either case the cause and effect were the same – When the gods saw what they'd begotten in their blind ravenous lust, what else could they say? And what could their myriad *creations*, propelled forth on a great spurt of divine jissom into the fertile womb of the cosmos – What else could they possibly think or do on arrival? And once they saw what *they* in turn begot, there was certainly no question as to what their options were in the face of such horror...

Ashes to ashes, lust to lust.

Goddamnit this whole fucking thing is fucked!

49.

Ed went back to the typewriter that night confused, dead sober, and with a very much renewed sense of purpose. Seeing now that his client was completely bat shit insane, he realized that it no longer mattered what he wrote about them, however outlandish or bizarre – they would believe it, and they would pay him for it. So, he loaded up a fresh sheet of paper and began reworking the entire thing.

To paraphrase what he wrote that night:

XXXX XXXXXXXX was born to XXXXXX and XXX XXXXXXXX on XXX XXth, 19XX CE in XXXXXXXXXX, XX, a small town known for its flagging textile industry. Mr. XXXXXXXX worked as a traveling salesman while Mrs. XXXXXXXX stayed home to raise XXXX and his twin sister, Eve.

Eve, being XXXX's identical twin, shared much in common with her older brother. Aside from their distinctive physical characteristics (red hair, blue eyes, sharply pointed canine teeth), they both harbored a great interest in the worlds to be found in books and in nature.

Editorial

But whereas XXXX wanted nothing more than to read and play all day, Eve had made it her personal goal to become the first female president of the United States by their Xth year.

At the age of X, while playing with his sister near the railroad tracks running through part of their property, XXXX sustained a head injury which left him partially amnesiatic. While this wouldn't ordinarily have been so debilitating to a child so young – practically a tabla rasa to begin with – XXXX would go on to suffer from persisting memory problems throughout his formative years. Eve would be instrumental in helping him to learn and relearn many things in this time.

Sadly, when he was only XX years old, XXXX would lose Eve and both his parents in a terrible motor vehicle accident while returning home from a family vacation. The sole survivor of the crash, XXXX was found wandering down the highway by local authorities, miraculously unharmed. He was later adopted by an aunt and uncle from a neighboring state, who brought him to live with them in their rural desert home.

The arid plateau nevertheless proved fertile ground for XXXX's imagination to take root in, with its exotic flora and fauna, surrounded by majestic mesa landscapes in which the child would act out stories from the books he'd read (when he could remember the details) and others he invented himself.

Years later, in his Miami apartment, XXXX reminisced upon this trying time:

"Things were hard after the death of my sister, who was also my best friend, you know. But somehow I found renewed life in that desert, dead and dried up as things were out there... For someone with a condition like mine, every day was full of discovery, experiencing things as if they were new each time."

But without Eve to keep him company, and no cousins with which to share his adventures, XXXX soon grew lonely and prone to bouts of depression.

"There were times when I would pretend as though Eve were still alive. With the two of us looking and sounding as alike as we did growing up – I hate to have to admit this because it's kind of embarrassing – but there were times when I would play her role in addition to my own."

As his depression grew worse and worse, XXXX found himself increasingly subject to such delusions, and it wasn't long before his behavior at home and school became somewhat… erratic. When his aunt and uncle sent him to the Greyson School for Boys following his expulsion from the local high school, XXXX's response was to run away from home.

From there he made his way to Reno, Nevada, hitching rides and prostituting himself for money along the way (sometimes as Eve and sometimes as himself).

"Easiest money we ever made," he says with a grin.

But after months of wandering from state to state, XXXX grew tired of the adventurous life he'd previously longed for. To make matters worse, his condition had degenerated to the point where he was beginning to forget even the most basic protocols of human etiquette, and his personal hygiene had sunk to the level of a common animal. After serving a short stint of jail time for prostitution and an unfortunate incident at the reptile house of the Reno Zoo, XXXX was ready to return home. Upon agreeing to finish his diploma at Greyson and resume taking his medication, XXXX was allowed to move back in with his aunt and uncle, where he would stay under their care until he was ready to leave for college the following year.

"I learned some pretty valuable life lessons out there on the road, but most of all I learned that the treatment I needed, just to function as a normal human being, was a little too expensive for me to afford on my own... Besides, whenever I could remember who they were and where they lived, I was beginning to miss my family!"

At university XXXX majored in zoology, with an emphasis on the various species of venomous and non-venomous snakes native to the American southwest. In addition to this core concentration, he would also graduate with a minor in Buddhist philosophy, a doctrine he had first been introduced to by a fellow traveler of the road. Following school, XXXX would even postpone his zoology career for a stint in the merchant marine, which allowed him to visit various ports of call in Asia – the birthplace of his adopted religion – as well as many other countries around the world.

"At the time I felt that, as much as I was still interested in animals, there was still so much to learn about the world's people, its places and cultures."

On an extended shore leave in Bangladesh, XXXX scheduled a two week journey to the mountains of Tibet which would ultimately last for two and a half years. Though this would mark the end of his career as a merchant mariner, it afforded him the opportunity to further his study and practice of eastern philosophy in a setting conducive to it. And furthermore, after all that time spent meditating on the circularity of existence and the great empty void within, it was this fortuitous delay that would allow him to meet his future wife, Lavinia, on his return voyage to the United States.

Dutch by birth, Lavinia had been educated in New Delhi at the behest of her wealthy parents. At the time she met XXXX, she was traveling to America in search of work and citizenship, defying her father's insistence that she return home to take over the family ice cream empire instead.

"I always used to call her my 'Queen Lavinia', which she hated."

At the age of XX, XXXX and Lavinia were married in Washington DC, where they purchased the home in which they would raise three children together. Lavinia was able to start a successful home business while XXXX finished his doctorate and taught zoology at Georgetown University.

It was also during this time that XXXX made the discovery of a lifetime. While doing research on a small chain of islands off the coast of Florida, he was able to catalogue five previously undiscovered reptile species – two lizards and three snakes. And as if this weren't remarkable enough, each of them were found to share many genetic characteristics with mammals of the mainland, including humans! Hermaphroditic and able to engage in sexual reproduction with itself as well as any other member of its species, *Bumwot serpentes* – the hair-covered snake – was perhaps the most remarkable of all.

As for how these evolutionary oddities came into being, it was correctly hypothesized that their development had been brought about by pollution from NASA's space program, centered at Cape Canaveral just thirty miles away. Whereas the island had previously been inhabited by your average run of the mill snakes, tree toads, and geckos, there must've been something in all

Editorial

that space rocket exhaust which caused them to mutate. XXXX would spend the rest of his professional career studying the curious animals which replaced them.

Toward the end of his tenure, the world renowned zoologist grew somewhat eccentric, publishing a paper that claimed a direct genetic lineage between reptile and mammalian species. Though not a new theory by any means, this version went so far as to suggest that mankind could find its earliest ancestors, not in the jungles of Africa, but in the serpents which came slithering out of the Garden of Eden following original sin. Needless to say, his findings were not heralded as particularly scientific, and as a result he was compelled to resign from the realm of academia.

Happily retired at the age of XX, XXXX found more time than ever to pursue other interests. While he continued in his own independent studies, he also rediscovered his long-neglected wife and one of their shared interests – camping.

"My parents left me this old school bus they'd towed up into the high dessert, after they died... I don't know where they found it or how they ever got it up there, but it sat on this ridge that gave the most amazing views of the surrounding countryside... That was always one of our favorite camping spots."

Unfortunately, this renewed passion for the outdoors would ultimately lead to tragedy. On their final camping trip to the bus in southern Utah, XXXX was struck by lightning in a freak electrical storm – an accident which left him confined to a wheelchair.

Though she tried her best to support her recently stricken husband, Lavinia filed for divorce only one year later. The depression XXXX had struggled with his entire life grew increasing worse, and his memory lapses became more and more frequent. And as if this weren't bad enough, it often seemed as if he'd become someone else altogether – any day could bring forth a new persona. Interestingly, however, it was neither his disability nor his growing eccentricity that eventually prompted the split between them. Rather, on the night of XXX, 20XX, XXXX suddenly and inexplicably attempted to murder Lavinia as she sat knitting in bed.

"And we'd had such a lovely day…"

50.

The following night, Ed presented this revision to his client.

"What is *this*?"
"Your life story. The one you asked for."
"But it's…"
"…not what you expected?

51.

NEO NUEVA NEW YORK, NY, 58XX CE – The city streets are abuzz with the mid-day lunch rush as Paul Duvall crosses the busy downtown street. Pushing his way through the swarming sidewalk crowds, he gets in line at the end of the restaurant queue, which is long enough extend well beyond the front entrance. Outside,

Editorial

above the building's glass double doors, is a large, brightly lit neon sign:

WANG'S CHINESE

He orders his food and sits down at an empty table. Damn he was hungry...

Unfortunately, the copy boys at the daily newspaper he worked for were pretty much bottom rung as far as job perks went – their boss only allowed them a measly half hour lunch for the entire ten hour day. Of course there were always articles coming in ready to be proofed, and no matter how fast they read (don't read *too* fast or you'll miss a typo!), they never seemed to catch up. Anyway, the point was that Paul needed the job, and as long as he needed it, he needed to be there working – it wasn't as if he were indispensable, not as a lowly copy boy, anyhow...

Some day, he hoped to make editor.

While he waited for his food, he tried to mentally organize the work he'd have to complete by the end of the day in order to make it home in time to get a good night's sleep. There were about 12 features that had to be proofed before three that afternoon, 15 more to get done by six that evening, and 20 or so new features coming in that night which would have to be read before the galley proofs were printed in the morning... Of course, this wasn't counting the inevitable corrections, retractions, and insertions that were bound to come in at the last minute.

Eventually, the waiter came with Paul's food, which he'd scented before it had even left the kitchen.

"Your order, sir," said the waiter as he approached the table.

Paul's long, sticky tongue had the first morsel in his mouth before the dish was even set down before him.

"Enjoy your flied lice."

Made in the USA
Lexington, KY
06 March 2010